LOVE-ACT

Mr Fox was no ordinary customer. Since Shirley had drifted into prostitution from an over-zealous middle-class upbringing, she had come to recognize them all: the first-timers, the talkers, the lookers, the hard guys, even the occasional psychopath. She liked to have control over her clients, but Fox was too intriguing to pass up, even if he was a crank. She was getting bored and anyway she could always change her mind at the station.

The ad had said 'Acting ability and discretion essential'. There was nothing new about that, wasn't that what the game was all about? But then came that first envelope with the rail ticket and cheque, the obscure Penguin paperback, and three-page script, accompanied by polite instructions to be on the 11.32 Brighton-to-London dressed like a drama student. After that she was even more confused. Was it just a scripted pick-up? Or perhaps some bizarre kind of God-game?

It was extraordinary how quickly after that first encounter with Fox Shirley gave up trying to work out her client's motives. Who ever heard of a punter who quoted T. S. Eliot or arranged meetings at the Tate? She had her performance to think of and besides it was fun. It was challenging and tantalizingly innocent. Soon Shirley was terrified of losing Mr Fox.

Love-Act toys with the reader's curiosity right to the very end. It could be a book about seduction and manipulation or truth and invention or desire and the end of desire. Or not. It is for the reader to discover where the conundrums of M. E. Austen's taunting game can lead in a first novel of rare and compelling ingenuity.

The author. M. E. Austen was born in 1951 in Warwickshire, where he also grew up. Since completing university at Leeds he has worked as a teacher of English as a Foreign Language in England and in Senegal, Finland and Portugal. He is at present living in Norwich. *Love-Act* is his first published work.

M. E. Austen

LOVE-ACT

JONATHAN CAPE
THIRTY BEDFORD SQUARE LONDON

The author and publishers are grateful to Faber and Faber for permission to reproduce three lines of 'Burnt Norton' from *Four Quartets* in *Collected Poems* 1909–1962 by T. S. Eliot. The line 'Nothing, like something, happens any-where' is from 'I Remember, I Remember' in *The Less Deceived* by Philip Larkin, published by The Marvell Press.

First published 1982
Copyright © 1982 by Michael Austen
Jonathan Cape Ltd, 30 Bedford Square, London

British Library Cataloguing in Publication Data
Austen, M. E.
  Love-act.
  I. Title
  823'.914[F] PR6051.U/

ISBN 0 224 02014 5

Phototypeset in Linotron 202 Plantin by
Western Printing Services Ltd, Bristol
Printed in

To Pat

Dear love, for nothing less than thee
Would I have broke this happy dream,
   It was a theme
For reason, much too strong for phantasy,
Therefore thou waked'st me wisely; yet
My Dream thou brok'st not, but continued'st it;
Thou art so true, that thoughts of thee suffice,
To make dreams truths, and fables histories;
Enter these arms, for since thou thought'st it best,
Not to dream all my dream, let's act the rest.

John Donne, 'The Dream'

One

For a long time he sat there unsure how to begin. On his desk were an ashtray and a paper-weight, some blank sheets of paper and a bottle of ink. A pen rested on one side of the ashtray. There was nothing else. He unscrewed the cap of the pen and idly examined the tip. A piece of hair had lodged in the nib and he spent some time trying to pinch it out. When that was done he replaced the cap. For a while he gazed at the window and drummed his fingers on the table. The he thought about having a cigarette. At last he pushed his chair away and stood. He yawned and scratched his head. Wearily, he wandered over to the bed and lay down. A spring twanged and the counterpane which had only been half on the bed now slipped to the floor. He put his hands to his forehead and closed his eyes to think. Five minutes, no more; then he had to admit there was no excuse. With a sigh, he got up and rerned to the desk. A short while later he had started to write.

Two

The first thing you should know about Mr Fox is that he was not a psychopath. Not in the usual sense at least. Had he been one of those I most certainly wouldn't have had anything to do with him. In this glorious profession, we dread the psychopaths more than any of the others.

Fortunately I learned what to look out for early enough. They are not at all how most people imagine them. For a start, they do not look the way they appear to in identikits – those are the distortions of hindsight: they don't have harelips, they don't have repulsive deformities of the body, and they don't have mean little eyes set too closely together. Neither do they nervously finger knives that have been left lying around, nor hold matches till the tips of their fingers are burned. They look just the opposite: quite harmless; the kind you might dream of having as a son. In fact, most seem quite sweet; doe-eyed – eyes are always the last clue to a man – and thoughtful; considerate; at pains to please. But they are absolutely dangerous. They are the ones you must get rid of as soon as you possibly can. I encountered two and I was very badly shaken up both times.

The first one smashed up the flat. He did not begin the moment he walked in, but some time later. He even gave warnings. He had seemed normal enough, he was even handsome in a boyish sort of way and, if I'm absolutely honest, I was quite looking forward to seeing what he was like. He didn't say much, but then that doesn't tell you anything – a lot of them don't, at least not until afterwards and then you can't shut them up. But he was very precise, very ordered about the way he undressed and a bit disconcerted when he couldn't see a hanger on which to put his jacket. He was polite too. I didn't have to ask him for the money – he asked me quietly where he should put it and when I answered he handed it to me as meekly as a lamb. Very soft-spoken; altogether very nice.

The problems did not start till we were in bed. Perhaps I should have realized before then. He lay down too carefully, as if he were stretching himself out on to an operating table instead of a bed, as if it were all a rite of some kind and we had to keep silent. It threw me a little – not much though – I was just a bit disappointed. I suddenly thought: I'm not going to enjoy this after all, but well, so what?

Even then there weren't problems immediately. I knelt beside him on the bedspread and began stroking my hair down his body. He had a good figure: no flabbiness or paunch. He kept in shape. And he was clean. But he lay absolutely still, looking up at the ceiling and avoiding my eyes whenever I glanced at him, all very cold and clinical, like patient and nurse. Nevertheless, from the other evidence it seemed that he was enjoying what he'd paid for so I took him in my hand. He did not move but he moaned a little as I worked at him. For a while he seemed to relax.

It was when I went down on him that the trouble started. He just said very quietly, 'Don't do that.' Quite firmly, but without raising his voice. 'Don't do that, please.' I don't know what possessed me then. I should have obeyed him right away but I thought I knew all the tricks there were to know; I sensed that in a strange way he wanted me to go on, and I was irritated by the sight of him lying there like that, so I said, 'Why? Don't you like it?' and went on licking him. He did not answer. I

9

continued. 'Most men do,' I said. 'I do.' I leered at him. I can't remember the precise words I used after that but I didn't stop. I started saying what a lovely thing he had got, how big and hard it was and how much I liked it – all the usual stuff they like to hear. He was muttering all the while but I couldn't make out what he was saying, and besides, having been told to stop, I was absurdly determined to go on. It was just as I was half-congratulating myself that I had known better, that he had wanted this after all – feeling him beginning to squirm beneath me – it was then, just as I thought he was coming to his climax, that I heard what he was saying: 'Filthy. Filthy lady. Filthy lady. Filthy.' Repeating it time after time, getting louder. And yet I still carried on. I'd had enough warnings.

He never came. One moment he was on the bed, the next he had leapt up and had started smashing things. It was not just the odd plate or glass – he completely wrecked the place, ripping the sheets in half, tearing up the carpet, crashing chairs against the wall as if they were matchwood. For almost five minutes he was berserk, totally out of control. All the time he kept shouting the same thing: 'Filthy! Filthy!', spitting the words out each time he hurled a new object at the wall.

What saved me was that I didn't scream or try to stop him. It was pure intuition. In some odd twisted way I'm sure he had forgotten that I was there, he was so lost in his violence. If I had got in his way I can't bear to think what might have happened. He could quite easily have snatched me up and crashed my head against the wall till it was pulp, or just broken my neck with one flailing swipe. But I simply cowered in the corner too horrified to scream and watched while he burnt himself out.

For that is what finally stopped him. It was pure exhaustion in the end. He was spent. He overturned the bed in one final frenzy, then stood there gasping for breath, occasionally kicking out at some bottle or tin that had fallen. Then he leant against the wall and began to cry.

From then on it was more pathetic than anything. After five minutes he was pleading with me not to be angry, asking me to hold him. I helped him dress and told him it was nothing to worry about yet even at the end when I managed to get him out of the door he was still sobbing. I didn't think he would come back, but I moved flat immediately afterwards just in case. I was almost penniless but it was worth it for the peace of mind.

I never discovered how the second one got my name and address but I didn't need any warnings: I recognized him in time. Perhaps he fitted the usual image more closely, perhaps not, but in any case the moment I opened the door he made me feel nervous. He was a small wiry type, very tightly wound. He hadn't rung the outer bell for me to open the main entrance and I didn't hear him on the stairs. He just said 'Shirley?' very quietly and then stood back in the shadows so that I couldn't see his eyes. Maybe if he hadn't done that I wouldn't have thought twice about letting him in, but the calmness, the slowness, the over-controlled way he had spoken my name tripped some alarm and suddenly I was terrified. From that second it was touch-and-go. At first my voice wouldn't come. Then I said, 'Shirley's moved.' He looked at me. There had been too long a pause between his question and my answer. I felt my bowels go loose. 'When?' he asked. He did not move out of the shadows. 'A week ago,' I said. The door to the flat was wide open. All my cosy long-established decorations and ornaments were clearly visible over my shoulder and I panicked. 'Er . . . no, a month ago – it must have been a month ago – yes,' I said weakly. He shifted his weight from one foot to the other and swayed into the light for a moment. It was obvious in his eyes that he didn't believe me. They narrowed slightly and he sighed. You don't forget whether it is a week or a month since you have moved into a flat, but it was too late by then. I felt myself sweating, thought I might faint. His hands were gloved and they hung limply down by his sides. 'And you live here now, do you?' 'Er . . . yes,' I said. 'Yes I do.' He paused. 'And where does Shirley live now?' 'I don't know,' I said. 'She didn't leave an address.' Again he shifted to the other foot, then looked down at his gloves. 'That's a pity,' he said. 'A great pity. I've come a long way to see her.' And he sighed again.

I don't pray very often, but I did then. I said to myself, 'Dear

Lord, if you do exist, get me out of this.' The man was standing there staring back at me. 'I'm sorry,' I said. There was a moment's silence. He seemed to consider everything that had been said, then nodded reluctantly. It was not a nod of thanks, more of acknowledgment – as if he were saying: 'All right, I give in. I know who you are, but you clearly know who I am too, so there's no point in going on.' As if the game would only work with an unsuspecting victim. He gave me one final swift look, then began to move off down the steps, heavily.

Immediately, I stepped back into the flat and swung the door closed behind me. Even then I did not feel able to breathe. I leant back against the door with my ear hard up against the wood and listened. It was one of those moments you only read about. I could hear no footsteps, knew that he had stopped on the stairs. I could tell he was weighing up the danger, deciding whether to come back up and ring once more. He went down a few steps and stopped. 'Please God,' I said again. Then the footsteps started coming up. He stopped just the other side of the door. 'Please God, I'll do anything,' I muttered. I could feel him listening there, only a few inches away on the other side of the door, listening for sounds from inside the flat. Again, I didn't know what to do. If I moved he'd know that I had been up against the door, if I kept silent he'd know that I was listening. I thought: if only I'd had the TV on, been listening to the radio.

And then at last there was the scratch of grit under his shoes as he twisted round and started back down the stairs. This time he did not stop. I heard him turning on the landings and then finally the dull thump of the outer door closing.

For five minutes more I did not move, convinced it was a trick. Then I slid down the door into a heap and wept. After that experience I did not leave the flat for three days. I'm sure he would have knifed me.

But Mr Fox was not like either of those two; not at all. As I have said, he was not a psychopath – he was dangerous of course, just as dangerous in a sense, but in a different way. Mr Fox was weird. A crank. It took me a very long time to work him out.

What I'm trying to explain is that there are definite types. You learn to recognize them. You must, in fact – and not only those psychopathic ones whom it is essential to know in time for safety's sake – but all the types. You *must* know them all, it's part of the business; if you didn't learn to pick them out you would never be very good. It's the art: telling who the first-timers are, who the so-called tough guys are, the lonely ones, the whole lot. They don't like to have to tell you. You're expected to know it yourself.

The easiest to guess are the first-timers. More often than not they tell you, but they don't need to – it would be less obvious if they had it written up in flashing lights. They fidget with their clothes, that's the first thing. Then they watch. If you meet them in a bar they watch you for hours, order drink after drink. You can almost hear them saying to themselves: 'Is she or isn't she?' over and over. It really gets on my nerves. At first, when I didn't know much, I occasionally waltzed over to them and said something like, 'Well, have you made up your mind?'or 'Are you ever going to ask me if I want a drink?' Well, very occasionally: I was rarely as sarcastic as that but the point is, whatever you say, whether you're sweet or tarty, if you speak it almost always scares them off. You simply have to wait. There is no point in trying to rush it. They are running through some tedious moral argument, one which they must resolve on their own, and if you try and force the issue, they're not ready. You just have to wait, to sit and suffer the endless hours of glances and twitches. Of course, sometimes they suddenly dash off, but often as not they finally lurch over to you and get you the drink.

When you don't meet them till they come to the flat, it's hilarious. There they nearly always say something like, 'Er . . . oh, I'm sorry . . . I'm not quite sure if I've come to the right place.' As if they're trying to find a long-lost aunt. They're so nervous. You have to relax them ––not with alcohol because the glass-trembles on make then worse ––but with a quick hand-job. You might expect them to leave directly after that, but it's odd, they never do. They are a little ashamed I suspect, they feel they have to prove themselves to you: they are afraid of what you might think. As though we cared. A little later they are ready for the whole works.

The tough guys are fairly easy as well. When you start in the business you invariably think that they are going to be the problem ones, but it's not the case at all. They are like chocolates or marshmallow cakes — hard on the outside but inside soft and sweet. They want mothering, to be held tight. Of course they would never tell you this — that's just the point — but they want to be loved, to be whispered to, to be clutched to your breast. It always reminds me of holding a baby — and that's nearer the mark than you might think — they're not really interested in anything but your tits. I'm not suggesting that they can't manage the rest, but it's just going through the motions, they're just getting the dirty water out of their system. They are very quick, very unskilful, and very easy to upset.

And yet they are generous, and in a sense, faithful. If they like you they come back, bring presents, perhaps even take you out. They're not stingy when they pay either. They carry their money in their back pockets in a great wad of notes, peel off a couple or whatever you ask and then a couple more so that you can 'get a dress'. Very sweet.

Next you've got the lonely ones. They often just want to talk. They don't know what they want to talk about, they just want to talk. And they are extremely apologetic. They are sorry that they've come, sorry to be taking up your time (they'll pay of course, you understand), they are sorry to be boring you (you must have heard this sort of thing a hundred times), sorry that they have this problem which they'll tell you about another time. They are very sorry, the sorry ones.

And then all the others. The lookers. The blow-jobs. The ones who can't get it up. There are the moaners and groaners, the ones who only want to talk about their wives. There are those who fold their trousers and carefully remove their watch. Others who like your name. Men who take all the loose change out of their pockets and put it in a tidy pile on the table. And the drunks. All sorts; the list is endless. The whole glorious range of manhood. You learn to recognize them, and to detest them. Like anyone who serves the public. Performs a service.

But Mr Fox was not like any of those. He did not fit any of those groups. Not the hard-guys, the talkers, the lookers or the drunks. Nor even the psychos. He was totally different. As I said, he was a weirdo. A crank.

Three

Right from the moment that the train rattled over Battersea Pier Bridge I suspected that I was escaping. I think it must have been the old thing of crossing water that did it, but as I peered down through the heavy metal struts at the Thames moving sluggishly beneath I felt that I was passing into a new country, leaving the familiar. Journeys always seem important, whatever your destination. I always think you feel special as a traveller, whereas watching other people travel makes you feel insignificant. I wonder where they are going and why, and I always believe that they must be on some terribly crucial mission to be flying along so full of determination to get where they are going. I felt important then, on that journey. I sat up close to the window watching excitedly as we slipped out of London. Those strange indelible scenes, like stills from a film: on Wandsworth Common, a man hurling a stick and the dog chasing after; or a football looping silently through the air. It was sunny, a warm spring day. I felt good.

Admittedly I was only going to Brighton, but I had business there. I had to meet someone, he had paid for my journey and I had a job to do. It was something different. Of course, I was sure there would be nothing very different about the service I eventually performed, but it was not the usual arrangement: it was quite out of the ordinary. I suppose I was excited really, for the first time for as long as I could remember, keyed-up because I was not quite sure what would happen. But there was also that other sense I first felt going over the Thames, of escape.

I loved every minute of that journey. I can remember it vividly. At Gatwick the runway is at right-angles to the line, and as we flashed past there was a jet on the tarmac, about to take off. It was already moving, but because it was coming straight at us it seemed only to quiver, as though it were stationary and just rocking slightly. Its take-off lights shone brilliantly even in the daylight and when the nose tipped up it was extraordinary, much longer and bigger than I had imagined. The whole sleek shape seemed to have to struggle into flight, clutching at the air for a second, then finding its grip. We had left it well behind before it crossed the line, but I can still see perfectly the moment it quivered on the runway. After that there were the South Downs rising and dipping away from the track, fields startlingly green after London, comfortable farms, cattle lumbering away from the wire.

Everything was so fresh and new. I kept leaning back towards the window to take in all I could, panning across the countryside, somehow hoping that I would never forget. I tried to work out how long it was since I had been out of London – certainly over a year. I wondered how I had managed to stand it – the stuffiness, the ponderance of the atmosphere, the sticky dirty feeling on the neck of your dress. It was a release, and yet something more.

It was only when we arrived at Brighton that I finally managed to place the sensation. The brakes tightened suddenly and the carriages jerked and everyone began to wake up. I sat there watching as people started to gather their bags and shuffle into life. There was a kind of weary sigh and a renewed rush of chatter. The next moment the train lurched to a halt and the doors swung open. It was after that, as I stepped out of the carriage and tasted the sea-air on my tongue for the first time, that I knew what the sensation had been all along: of coming on holiday as a small child, the promise of sand and sunshine, the brief spell of freedom.

I was born in 1958 in Coventry. It was a pretty miserable place. It had been very badly blitzed in the war, most of the centre had been completely destroyed and when it was rebuilt the city became totally characterless despite the wonderful new cathedral I was meant to feel so proud about. I remember when I was at school one of the more enlightened teachers read us a poem which mentioned the place. It was written by someone quite famous, though I can't recall his name; he had been born there as well and was revisiting it in the poem. I don't remember much of it now but one line has stuck in my mind and pretty much sums it up. 'Nothing, like something, happens anywhere.' I rather like that. Well, it wasn't quite true in my case, but I feel more or less the same about the place as he did. I was never very happy and I never go back. It is a non-place.

We lived in a good, solid, middle-class semi-detached. It had pebble-dashed walls and a wrought-iron front gate that I was always being told off for swinging on. Next door lived the Williamsons and on the other side, Mrs Bryant. Her husband had left her before we came to live in the street and she would occasionally have men-visitors, so I was not allowed to speak to her, though it was never really explained to me what she had done wrong. She had a spotty son called Timothy; I used to throw stones at him by standing on the dustbin.

In our house, dear father ruled the roost. To say that I dislike him would be an understatement. On occasions, in my more objective moments, I think I can understand what produced his resentment, but it doesn't change my feelings – it's just an explanation.

By rights (he was always talking about rights), he should have been a bank manager. But he wasn't. That was the dreadful affliction that had crippled him, nothing more. For twenty-five years he had worked in the same branch on the outskirts of the city, and for twenty-five years he had been consistently passed over for promotion. He never stopped thinking about it. Each year he would watch a novice enter and settle, then leap-frog above him, and it left him with a pathological hatred of young people. This he chose to inflict by becoming a Sunday-School Superintendent – God knows why he happened on that particular post from which to take his vengeance: he wasn't really religious.

Nevertheless, every Sabbath the whole family would be filed out of the house and seated in his precious 1100 and, with him at the wheel of course, the stately procession to the chapel would begin. Now, whenever anyone utters the word 'father' that is the vision which rears up in my mind: not his goggle-eyes or stupid swollen face, but for some reason, the back of his head and the livid purple patch at the base of his neck that I used to stare at the whole of the journey.

He was, of course, a good father. Oh, yes. He didn't beat us, he didn't take the slipper or the belt to us and he always gave us our pocket-money regularly – on a Saturday evening, when the shops were closed. I imagine he thought the Sunday would give us time for mature reflection, we would not be able to rush straight out and fritter it away on sticky sweets or silly records – and we were given little red notebooks to note down our expenditure. We had to take them to him to be checked once a month – as I have said, he worked in a bank.

Occasionally during Sunday lunch, after a particularly stimulating sermon in the morning, he would deliver lectures to us on subjects such as 'The World as I see it', 'The Trouble with Modern Youth', or 'What the Lord said but was somehow omitted from the Bible'. And incredible though it might seem, we listened to him. I believed in him. He was the final arbiter in everything, his opinions could not be disputed, his pronouncements were unquestionable. Now, of course, I see exactly what he was. He was a bigot and a hypocrite. He was cold and unloving. He was not truly interested in anyone but himself. Especially my mother.

Poor Mum, she never stood a chance. She was not allowed to

be a person. In his scheme of things she was a mother to her children and a wife to him; she was not permitted any other existence. His moral righteousness did not leave room for her to be anything else. He moulded her into exactly what he wanted her to be: a home-loving housewife, a sort of nodding sheep-dog, nuzzling at his side. She was mute except for platitudes, muzzled most of the time. She was only expected to grunt agreement with what he said. At one time I used to think that I would love to have seen her before she met my father, but now I don't – he had managed to catch her before she had developed a mind for herself, she was domesticated too young.

However, my sister and I – I was the elder – were treated differently. We were 'young people' and he would make sure we didn't 'go wrong'. After all, he had had us from birth, for Christ's sake; he could do anything he wanted with us. He wanted two sweet automatons.

We both worked hard and did well at school. We had bright shiny satchells, garters to hold up our socks and pigtails down our backs. We held our arms up straight to answer questions and we did not fool around. Father was well pleased. The only thing that slightly marred the picture, so to speak, was when they found I needed glasses. My father was a little put out – he was always referring to them; I think he was vaguely hurt, it spoilt the cosy picture and reflected on him somehow: it suot be quite perfect, that he had not divulged some appalling hereditary taint. No doubt he blamed my mother's side – her brother Harry was almost blind.

That apart, for seventeen years of my life things ran without a hitch. Then I got pregnant.

They say it always happens to the sweet innocent ones; well, I don't know. I certainly was anyway. Thinking back I'm amazed to believe that I was actually allowed to have a boyfriend; maybe dear father imagined a bit of that kind of tolerance would make him a perfect modern parent. Whatever the case, I was so surprised, so shocked to be allowed out after ten, and above all so desperate to keep my boyfriend, that I was prepared to let him go further than all the other girls would have done. They all said that they 'did it' of course, which they didn't, but I believed them all the same. It was the classic case. One night, contorted in the back of his father's Cortina, poor David spurted his hot little come inside me almost without my realizing and it was done. I was in the sixth form just coming up to 'A' Levels, with a place at Durham to read History virtually certain.

I did not tell my mother for two months. As each sickening day passed the reality of what had happened seemed to grow simultaneously both worse and more far-fetched. It was not possible – just that one time. It was against all the laws of averages, a one in a million chance, not a million to one. I became more and more confused. I could hardly speak. I was pale and trembling after the lack of sleep. Even at the end it wasn't really a conscious decision to tell her – she asked me what was wrong. The shock of it nearly killed her.

There was never any question that I would have the baby, of course. As soon as my father knew, there was nothing to discuss. I was totally bemused – I did not know what I wanted – in fact, I don't think I knew what was happening the whole time. I have strange recollections of saying delirious things such as I would have the baby, I would marry David (who had not offered), that we were hopelessly in love; but they were just standard utterances and besides, the matter was out of my hands.

With his usual efficiency my father had the abortion arranged within days. I was whisked off to a clinic in Birmingham and in a dose of anaesthetic that peculiarly unreal night's work was undone. I was back in the house almost before I realized I had gone. The idea that a human had been growing inside my body never occurred to me – at the time.

Throughout all this my father didn't say a single word to me. When he wished to communicate with me it was done through a go-between: my mother, of course. At least she was sympathetic. I realize now that it was probably the one time she had really stood up against him; she argued with him and insisted that I should be allowed to stay at home for the following two months until it was decided what was to be done with me. I was not consulted once. After the initial couple of days I did not cry, but sat around the house staring distantly at objects. The whole thing seemed to have happened to a completely different person.

What happened to David I don't know. I don't blame him. Of course it was his fault in a way, he should have had a condom I suppose, but neither of us was 'grown up'. If anything, I feel a bit sorry for him. I know that my father visited his parents and I can't bear to think what that was like; but Father was too much of a coward to have punched anyone on the nose. He probably just demanded the price of the abortion.

However, what really destroyed dear father was that is was impossible to avoid telling the school. Everyone else he could fob off with some woeful tale of sickness, but the school needed a certificate and he had to produce one. There was no way that the truth could be withheld, and as if that weren't crushing enough, the Headmaster attended the church. He was, at least temporarily, a broken man.

I was allowed to take my 'A' Levels (all of which I failed – I left one paper completely blank) but a short time after that I was no longer required in the house. I became a non-person, a daughter he'd never had.

His decision was that I should become a nurse. A training hospital in London was chosen and the news was imparted to me through my mother. 'Tell her that she's going to London. Tell the girl she'll be a nurse.' 'Your father says you're going to London. He says you'll be a nurse.' Just like that. Perhaps he felt that as a nurse my sin would be absolved – that was the way he thought – through healing others, he imagined, the horrible goring he had suffered might just possibly be cured. I did not feel anything in particular. As with all the decisions he made I did not question it. I applied for a place without protest. I have vague recollections of a pile of forms and an interview taking place, but the whole thing was arranged with extraordinary ease. I would go in a month. Then a week. I wandered dazedly round the house and packed a trunk. Then I left. What had happened didn't really come home to me until after the train had pulled out. My mother had been in tears on the platform while he waited in the car after carrying my bags. Had my mother been able to drive I don't think he would have even come to the station.

If my father hoped for my salvation, he didn't get it. My nursing career was never very distinguished: I was thrown out of nursing college near the end of my second year. The first time I was discovered with a man in my bed in the nurses' home it was only a warning. The second time it was different. No amount of pleading would have helped then, even if I had begged on bended knee to stay (which I didn't – I hated the old bags who ran the place) it would still have been out. I had developed quite a reputation.

It started slowly enough. I didn't understand for a long time that it was to spite my father, to get back at him, and indeed maybe at the very beginning it wasn't. I felt ugly in my glasses, unloved, totally lacking in confidence, an entirely worthless human being. I didn't even go to the first few nurses' dances, and then when I did I barricaded myself behind giggles and a cluster of shrieking virgins. Although I didn't like them, I was terrified without their protection: I was shy, poorly-dressed and mortally afraid of getting tipsy.

At Christmas, however, when I was not invited home, the first man made a foray into the den: it was a smash-and-grab raid, a one-night stand. I was drunk, but that wasn't the reason; I let him screw me because it made me feel less ugly, almost as a compensation to him. After that it wasn't so difficult. Very soon there was another. And another. The longest relationship lasted a fortnight, but it didn't seem to matter: each one I notched up made me feel even better. I got contact lenses and found that the time-lapses between the men grew even shorter. I was more assured, less dumpy, but not a great deal wiser. Very soon I was easy meat, a sure lay for anyone a bit desperate.

I wasn't fully aware of what was happening until the end of my first year. Then I noticed other girls muttering about me, shaking their heads in the corridors as I passed and I suddenly wondered what it was about. It took me some time to react. Even then it was nothing conscious, nothing that I had decided upon in advance. It happened quite by chance.

We had gone out for a drink, a group of us, with some blokes tagging along. I didn't know them but they obviously knew all about me and halfway through the evening I saw two of them whispering together, nodding in my direction. They were smirking stupidly at one another, drinking their beer rather too swiftly and I knew at once what was going to happen. A few minutes later, one of them, a rather greasy, lank-haired type with a little snub nose, sidled over to me. He asked me if I wanted a drink. I felt helpless. I accepted, thinking rather sickly that I had no choice but to be lumbered with him for the evening, for once not wanting to take anyone back. And he was just too quick – that's what did it in the end – he regarded it as a foregone conclusion, his right. Directly after that drink, as if by buying me that and offering me a cigarette he had staked some undisputable claim, he asked me straight out if we should go back to his flat. It came to me on the spur of the moment – I had not planned it at all – but I sort of shrugged my shoulders and answered, 'Why not?' Then, as soon as we were out of the pub, I turned to him and said, 'You haven't asked how much'. He was completely taken aback, speechless. I frowned. 'Didn't your friend tell you – it's a tenner you know.' He went white, still unable to speak. I put my hand on his shoulder and pretended to sound sympathetic. 'Oh dear,' I said, 'I think someone has pulled a fast one on you.' He began swearing softly. I felt extraordinary, suddenly supremely confident. I went on quickly before I could give myself time to think. 'Well, never mind anyway. But do you want to or not?' I think he was too embarassed to back down, would have been too ashamed to walk back into the pub. In the end he nodded dumbly and we went along to his flat. I demanded payment in advance. It gave me the most amazing kick – and, later perhaps surprisingly, my first orgasm as well.

After that I only did it for money. Of course it took me some time to build up a regular clientele – the second one was the bloke's friend interestingly enough – but in general they were just desperate types and the ones who thought it might make a change to pay for it. In a sense it was the best time of my life; I found it gave me an extraordinary thrill and a power over men – in fact, over people in general, for by some weird process of inverted logic the other girls found it awesome that I should be selling my body. There was always that strange romance about being a fallen woman.

But it couldn't last for long, even I knew that. As the rumours about me grew and as the carpet leading to my bedroom door became more well-trodden, it became only a matter of time before something happened. I realized it but could not stop myself. I think the prospect pleased me. One May night my door burst open and Matron and two of her cronies marched in while one of the poor blokes was doing his business. They did not look particularly shocked – after all, they already knew – but I did not attempt to cover myself up, I just lay there heaving helplessly with laughter. I was given twenty-four hours to get out, and the old bitch wrote to my parents. My father replied to me a month later saying, well confirming really, that I would never be welcome in the house again and that my mother had had a nervous breakdown.

The next period of three months or so was the only time that I went on the game just for the money: that is, when I had to in order to live. I sat around in bars and gave knowing smiles in hotel foyers, and for a time came close to the window-card stage, but my saving grace was that at school we had learnt typing and at last the bureau where I had registered found me some work. For almost a year after that I shared a flat with two other girls at the office, We were fairly close to the bread-line; but I did not supplement my income. I would like to say that it was out of respect for my mother but I think the truth is that it was impossible while sharing with the others. I even had a boyfriend but after a month he bored me. There was a brief affair with dope, which depressed me even more, and then I decided to move out. I changed jobs, going only part-time, and began building up my clientele again. For some odd reason that

I do not fully understand I told everyone at work that I was an unmarried mother and needed extra time for my daughter. I called her Sally and even went so far as to buy some snaps of a baby to hand around. Everyone showed great sympathy, which I took pains to brush aside. I suppose you could say my acting career had already started, though I did not see it like that at the time.

And for two years I had been living the same. I was earning more than enough to live on but not really going anywhere. By the time all this happened I was bored and depressed and something had to change. It did. The holiday in Brighton could almost have been planned.

When I left the station I did not immediately go to find a hotel but wandered down to the front. There, on the promenade, it was not warm – still too early in the year for the sun to have gained any real strength, and a steady wind flapped through my coat. All the same I sat down on a bench between the two piers and watched some workmen repainting the balustrade ready for the coming season – a turquoise green, bright and airy, a summer's colour. The wind tangled through my hair and streamed under my collar so that it rushed down my back making me shiver, but I did not mind. I felt recklessly refreshed, free to do exactly what I wanted, suddenly able to control everything about myself. I watched the seagulls strutting along the edge of the promenade and then wheeling off in the gusting currents of air, and tritely thought that like them I was perfectly free to choose exactly where and when I went. I felt a smile creeping across my face and determined that I was going to enjoy myself.

When it finally became too cold to sit any longer I took a brisk walk along the front, then scrambled down on to the shingle and tossed some pebbles at the waves. After that I went for a cup of coffee in a café overlooking the prom. My face was burning after the cold wind but I lingered there for an hour, warming, and gazed dreamily out through the window. Next I booked into a guest-house along the front, lay down on the bed and fell straight asleep.

It was seven o'clock before I awoke, and dark. I lay there for a little while wondering what I could do that evening, quite content, then got up and washed and went out to have a drink. The holiday mood had not left me and after half an hour I decided to move on and treat myself to an enormous steak. I found a place, ordered a half-bottle of wine, and finally emerged after an hour, bloated and flushed, with my mind made up to find myself a man.

It wasn't difficult to spot a rep drinking alone in a hotel bar. Later on I sneaked him into the guest-house. It was a little holiday fling; I did not take any money from him, we just had a fuck and went to sleep. I did it simply because it felt right, to keep up that sense of lightness, because I wanted to celebrate in some way. Christ knows what he thought; probably just surprise, but when we woke up the following morning I was glad. I told him I was here for a conference and had simply felt lonely, and he nodded wisely as if to say the same thing happened every night. At least he didn't ask me for an address or anything like that, he accepted it for what it was and left saying it had been 'nice'. Well, that's how I felt, although he wasn't anything special.

After breakfast I returned too my room and wondered what I should do until it was time to make my way to the station. I flipped through a magazine for a time and gazed out of the window, toying with the idea that I might move down to Brighton permanently. There was sure to be enough trade here in the summer and I was fairly confident I would be able to get some secretarial work. It would be a drag to have to build up all the contacts again; no doubt quite a lean time for a while, but why not? Nothing could be worse than my present situation. Yes, I would move down here, near to the sea, get out of stinking London.

Having settled that in my mind, I pulled out the script, thinking it might be wise to have one more look over my lines. It was quite a shock. As soon as I read the first few exchanges the craziness of the job and my fears came flooding back. For

27

twenty-four hours I had forgotten about it – since I'd arrived I'd not given Mr Fox a thought. I had felt excited enough, but in a general sort of way. I had put it all to the back of my mind, transferred my excitement to this holiday sense, tricked myself into believing it was something other than it was. Now when I saw it afresh it seemed totally different. It was absurd. The whole affair was lunatic. What was I doing here? Why had I travelled all the way down to Brighton? For what? I must have been out of my mind. I detected an ominously sick taste in the back of my mouth. At that moment, I decided that I would not have anything to do with Mr Fox under any circumstances. I would not go through with it.

Four

Mr Fox didn't contact me in the usual way at all. I have said he was different; well, he was even in that respect.

At the time that I saw his advert nearly all my business was arranged through contacts: I was what you might call a high-class tart. Only at the beginning of my career – the nursing college days – did I do cheap tricks. After that I moved up market; I never worked the kerb-crawlers and I never worked the pubs. Nor did I ever have a little card yellowing in some window – 'French lessons with Shirley', or anything corny like that. There was that one period when I was nearly forced to, I suppose, but I survived. I never had to stoop that low. Instead my business came by what I like to call 'recommendation'. There were a few hotel-porters and half-a-dozen taxi-drivers who expounded my worth, they selected for me, took a rake-off and I trusted them. It was quite lucrative. In addition to this, there was the old jungle-talk; that is, satisfied customers who were magnanimous enough to pass the word around and inform associates of their good luck. I didn't have to be choosy – they were all wealthy – but nevertheless if I didn't like the look of one it was too bad. I liked to think I worked for my benefit and not theirs, whatever they cared to believe; I had my other job as well and didn't desperately need the cash. They just had to stuff it if I wasn't in the mood. I did it for kicks. To be absolutely frank I liked to think of myself as that Jane Fonda character in *Klute* – a high-class call-girl, independent and professional, a bit special I suppose. I was never the powdered, perfumed, tap-room type of tart. Or so I thought.

To say that the novelty had worn off might sound ludicrous, but it had. I was simply fed up. It was becoming like any other job. God knows what I was looking for; I don't think I was conscious I was looking for anything in fact, but I was flipping through a magazine and there it was. It was on the back page: a little boxed advertisement, tucked away down amongst the sex-aids, the penis-developers and the massage parlours.

MODEL REQUIRED for special assignments.
Acting ability and discretion essential.
Apply, with photograph, Box 14.

That was all. There wasn't any more to it. No mention of money, none of the usual blonde/brunette nonsense – just that.

My first reaction was to laugh. Acting ability and discretion are the hallmarks of this profession. What exactly was so special about that? I remember that I didn't think any more about it for a while, but carried on idly browsing through the pages, even read one of the corny short stories. Yet when I'd finished I found I had turned to that back page again and was staring blankly at the little box.

'Special assignments'. The working had been designed to tease – like some obscure crossword clue or riddle it grew infuriating the more I thought about it. 'Acting ability' and 'discretion'. Why? What for exactly? What king of acting ability and what kind of discretion? It didn't make sense. Another read through made it no clearer. The advert had irritated me, caught my attention and now I couldn't get it out of my mind. The more I thought about it the more aware I was that I was becoming captivated. I think even then I knew that I would reply, but refused to admit the truth to myself. Finally I threw the magazine down on a chair and started fiddling around in the flat.

Half an hour later I was back at the magazine, checking once more that I had not mistaken the wording, or missed something out. I hadn't of course, I knew that before I went back to look. It was becoming an obsession simply because it was so obscure. What was it for? All kinds of crazy visions flashed through my head. Films, girlie magazines, really kinky stuff? It was clearly for a prostitute – 'model' only means one thing; but what about the rest? And 'photograph'. What kind? A nude shot or a portrait? Perhaps even a passport photograph?

It was just too absurd. I told myself that I must forget it and slung the magazine away in a drawer. When you examined it closely, what was there? Nothing. No real clues and no denials – just that a prostitute was required. Well I would most definitely forget it. I always liked to call the shots.

I posted my letter three days later, dropping it hurriedly into the box before I could give myself time to change my mind. It was just a short note: I asked for further details and enclosed a small photograph – a fairly neutral one, not a nude, pouting pose but just head and shoulders. I rather vainly thought my eyes had that mysterious smouldering look. He would have to imagine the rest.

I had given the thing a lot of thought. The day after I had first seen the advert I finally admitted to myself that there was no way I was going to be able to forget it, so I might just as well settle down and try to sort it out.

The first thing I wondered was whether I had after all misunderstood the meaning of the word 'model'. That was quickly dismissed. The type of magazine in which the advert had been published, the page, the position on that page, all these pointed to one interpretation only: that 'model' was a euphemism for prostitute as I had originally thought. Besides, no true model with any self-respect would answer an advert where 'discretion' was stipulated as one of the essential requirements.

So, what next? I considered all the possibilities I could think of. Girlie magazines were out. Acting ability could hardly be required for anything like that. But blue films, they were possible. It probably meant hard-core if it was suggested you should be discreet, very hard-core and very illegal in fact. Discreet would be a veiled way of saying this; after all you could hardly advertise for that sort of thing by saying that you had every intention of breaking the law. But then why mention it? Surely that subject would be more suitably broached at a later date – say, when money was being discussed. The phrase 'acting ability' didn't fit either. None of the blue films I had seen had needed any kind of acting ability at all – used in that context it was a joke. No, that couldn't be it. A live show then? Some kind of performance work? I felt I was getting a little closer to the truth. It was possibly some bar in Soho recruiting girls for a rather imaginative porno-show – a song-and-dance routine, some kind of glorified strip. But discreet? Once again it didn't quite fit.

The only other thing I could think of was kink. As a high-class tart I had steered well clear of it – the schoolgirl pigtails and tunic, the Nazi jackboots and horsewhip – all that kind of thing was out, I wanted nothing to do with it, and, perhaps rather surprisingly, I had rarely been asked. But I could imagine this advert was that: 'acting ability' might quite easily be the grand way they envisaged their particular fantasy – creative expression, *une pièce de théâtre*. As for 'discretion' – well, it would be someone of importance: a big businessman, a politician, or a wealthy lord perhaps. Briefly, I conjured up all kinds of hilarious scenarios: decadent scenes of ancient Rome, little dramas in a sultan's palace – all of which ended with some sad old man jerking off. Somewhat disappointedly I came to the conclusion that of all the possibilities this was the most likely; the only weak point in the theory was why he should bother to advertise in the first place – why didn't he simply ask?

Nevertheless, I replied. No harm could come of inquiring, I argued, and I could always back out.

I took a couple of precautions. After my experience with the two psychopaths I did not relish the idea of revealing where I lived before I knew a little more about the business or saw what he was like. If whoever had written the advertisement had stipulated 'discretion', then I was similarly entitled to safeguard myself. I gave a false name and address.

It took me some considerable time to devise a scheme which would work. I couldn't give any of my friends' addresses – not that I had many friends – since that would mean exposing them to the same risks, and apart from that I couldn't think of anywhere I could use as a holding address where my receipt of letters would not seem suspicious.

Finally, just as I was about to give up hope, an idea occurred to me: I could enlist Tom for help. Tom was the doorman-cum-porter at the office; and old fellow of about sixty, the kind of character with a quick answer for all the staff, and a compulsive flirt. I was on winking terms with him – just the usual silly nods and nudges, all perfectly harmless, but I suddenly thought that he would appreciate an intrigue and be prepared to play a part. He sorted the mail that came to the building and distributed it, and I was sure he wouldn't object to what I had in mind. I concocted a tale for him, explaining that I was stringing along an admirer and didn't want him to know my real name. The man would write to me, care of the office, thinking I was called Sylvia Rivers (the name I had decided upon); would Tom keep any mail that came for that name for me? He was overjoyed, apparently chuffed to have been let in on a secret and amused at my little plot. There were all kinds of wisecracks and head-shakings of course, but he swore to secrecy. The stage was then set, and all I had to do was wait. Vaguely, I felt a kind of smugness at my little trick; by the simple fact of using a false name and address I felt that I would be able to maintain control of whatever the business was.

Nothing came for over a week. Despite myself, each day I grew more and more hopelessly excited, torturing myself with doubts – should I have sent a different photograph, should I have replied at all? What if my letter had been too formal, too straight? Should I have made some lewd suggestion, or hinted at something rather more dubious than I had? Every morning I cornered Tom alone in the corridor and demanded by letter, but every morning his answer was the same: sorry, but nothing. His jokes and winks became more irritating each time.

And then at last, one Wednesday morning as I walked into the office, he winked, beckoned me over to the desk and secretively handed me a fat brown manilla envelope. I had virtually given up hope.

For a while that morning I tried to resist the temptation of opening it, telling myself that I would wait until I got home before examining the contents, but it was no good. In the end, like some dewy-eyed schoolgirl clutching a love-letter to her breast, I sneaked down to the toilets, locked myself in one of the cubicles and ripped open the envelope.

After I had looked at the contents I was even more confused. There were five things. I must have stared at them for about twenty minutes in all, gazing blankly as though I had to bring them back to mind for some peculiar memory game. I felt I had not progressed at all, I had no idea what it was all in aid of, I simply felt more nervous, more excited and more bewildered still. At last, realizing I had been away far too long, I had to stuff them back in the envelope and return to my typing. I would look at them later – the whole thing would become clear if I considered it calmly that afternoon.

When I got home I made a cup of coffee, lit a cigarette and laid out the five things on the table in front of me in order to examine them methodically. This time I would understand.

The first item was a return rail ticket to Brighton. I looked at it again to confirm what the letter had said. Sure enough, it was a seat reservation for the day that had been mentioned – and in a first-class compartment.

The second was a Penguin paperback. This time I examined it more closely, taking in the cover, the title and the author's name, but the only thing I recognized was the reproduction on the front – a Gaugin I guessed. I flipped the book over, and it was: a painting entitled 'Nevermore' – the same as that of the book. The author, Matthew Fowler, was not one I'd heard of and there was nothing written inside the cover. I shook the book once in case anything should fall out, but nothing did. I put it down and turned to the next item.

It was three pages of carefully, closely typed script, like a short play. In the toilet I had only glanced at it briefly, and it hadn't made any sense; this time I read it through completely and was still not enlightened.

The fourth thing was the letter, which I re-read. It was a single sheet of paper, once again typed, but without an address heading. The tone was abrupt and faintly unnerving.

Dear Ms Rivers,

Thank you for your inquiry. If you are interested in what I propose, please learn the enclosed script thoroughly.

On March 21st travel to Brighton and catch the 11.32 train back to London. Your seat has already been reserved and you will find the number on the ticket that is provided. The compartment will be empty except for one other occupant −—a man of about sixty years of age, dressed in a pale-grey suit. The rest of the details you will find in the script, but you will repeat the dialogue that you have learnt with this man. For your guidance I should tell you that you are a drama student in your early twenties, so please dress accordingly.

No doubt you will feel that you are entitled to further explanation −—I have my reasons for not giving you this and would ask you not to ask questions.

I trust that the enclosed cheque will be sufficient to cover your services and any expenses that you will incur.

If these arrangements are unsuitable, or if you do not wish to go further, please contact the magazine at Box 14 in good time before the 21st.

Yours,
P. FOX

There wasn't any more. I looked at the last item again – the cheque. It was for £100, signed P. Fox, and made out to Ms Sylvia Rivers. It served me right. When the other cheques for larger sums started arriving I had to open a bank account under my stage-name.

March 21st was over a fortnight away so I had plenty of time to think the matter over. I dithered for a week turning it over and over in my mind, but whichever way I looked at it, it was still absurd. I was being paid £100 – in advance – for what? A pick-up. There was no other way of describing it. However much I tried to read into it, it always came down to the same thing: a pick-up, a scripted pick-up perhaps, and pretty pretentious at that, but a pick-up nevertheless.

I must have read the script a hundred times. It was as he had described it. The girl is sitting on the train reading the book I'd been sent. Near the end of the journey she comes to the last page, closes the book and the man sitting opposite her asks her about it. They discuss it for a couple of minutes and then the subject is dropped. It is the familiar pattern. After a few minutes' silence, that initial barrier having been broken, he begins to ask her about herself and by the time they reach London he feels confident enough to invite her for a drink. For a time she acts the 'Oh-I-don't-think-I-ought-to' part but finally agrees of course and they scurry off to the pub. The script ended there. It was hardly original. – It didn't describe what was intended to take place after that, but it wasn't difficult to imagine, I decided. And yet that was it. The two characters didn't even have names: it just said 'MAN' and 'GIRL' typed in red, and then their lines given in black. He didn't even ask the girl her name.

However, the directions were extraordinarily detailed. Throughout the dialogue there were precise instructions as to what each should do or how the lines should be said. It might say something like *Girl closes book wearily*, or *Man leans forward and takes book*, and there would be bracketed notes such as (*with irony*) or (*amused*). It was exactly like a one-act play or what I

imagined a film-script might resemble: I could visualize the
episode as the start of a hundred films, the accidental encounter – but what followed? It was a pick-up, but why?

Once again I had to go over the possibilities. The live-show
idea, the Soho bar song-and-dance routine, was now excluded,
but what of films? Perhaps it was that after all 2 some kind of
candid camera set-up. The director wanted to see if I could act,
learn lines, play a part; the crunch would come in the pub; if I
didn't make a complete idiot of myself the man would say
something like, 'Youknowyoushouldbeinfilms – haveyourever
givenitanythought?' Andthenacoupleofdrinkslater, 'Look, I'll
comecleanwithyou – I'mafilmdirector. IthinkIcoulduseyou.
Whydon'tyoucomealongtomystudiothisafternoonandwe'llsee
how you shape on film?' I imagined this was the usual approach,
andthenthoughtagain. Itwascompletelywrong – theadverthad
madeitquiteclearwhatsortofgirlwasrequired,allhehadtodowas
to hbaked script at the studio, tell me to strip off to
seeifmytitswerebigenough,thenhaveadrinkanddiscussterms.
Thebusinessonthetrainwassounnecessaryforabluefilm. Ilooked
attheticketagain,thefirst-classseatreservation.Andthebook,for
Christ's sake. No, it could not be a film.

Reluctantly I turned my mind to the only other possibility I'd
considered – the crank. It was a case of the schoolgirl syndrome
after all: gym-slips and plaits – this time with a difference.
There'd be the little game in the train, a nervous drink in the
pub and then at long last he'd stammer out that he had
something to ask. Once more I tried to visualize it: he wouldn't
look at me, he'd be glancing round like a sparrow to see if there
were danger near. His scrawny legs would poke out his trousers
like sticks and his collar would be three sizes too large for his
neck. I'd have to suggest it to him in the end, he would be so
nervous ––but finally we would traipse back to the flat. I'd have
to guess at his particular fantasy and pump him for clues, but it
would finish with him on all fours crawling about the room,
trousers round his ankles. No, it was not for me. I'd heard
enough tales about pathetic old men. I decided I wouldn't go. I

detected a trace of sympathy for the poor man in my attitude, but my mind was made up. The trip was not on.

I picked up the cheque and waved it in front of my eyes. I would send it back to him. I wouldn't go, but neither would I take his money. And yet . . .

I read the letter for the umpteenth time. Travel to Brighton . . . catch the 11.32 train . . . your seat had already been reserved . . . learn the script thoroughly . . .

Polite but firm. Not the usual sort of old crank – he was pretty sure of himself, there was no mistaking that. He seemed to assume that having replied to the advertisement I was certain to come. The more I read it, the less I liked the tone. It was as if I didn't have any choice in the matter, as if it were all pre-ordained. No chance, Mr Fox, I said out loud. I don't like your little scheme. No one tells me what to do. No, I won't go, I said resolutely. I won't travel down to Brighton – and for another thing I'll keep the cheque.

Five

Almost sulkily I stuffed the script back into my bag and
wandered over to the window. It was dull; the sea stretched out
to the horizon flat and uninteresting, likeless without the
gusting wind of the previous day. Down on the promenade a
few people straggled slowly along by the rails, bored, filling in
time, and the gulls that only the day before had been wheeling
and banking steeply above my head were sitting stiffly on the
water rocking gently to and fro as the tide pulled them nearer
than farther from the shore. There was a purposelessness about
everything – yesterday everyone had seemed to be marching
about briskly, today it appeared they had nowhere to go, no
reason to do anything. I felt a heavy depression weighing down
on me, the holiday-feeling suddenly evaporating in a puff of
anti-climax.

Why had I come in the end? I remembered with shame how I
had determined not to come, told myself to pocket his money
and forget it. Why after that had I changed my mind? Looking
out over the dull lifeless scene I realized it had been pure
boredom. The script had given me something to do, somewhere

to aim. I had been prepared to have a go at anything for a little excitement. Like an aspiring young actress rehearsing for an audition, already dreaming that I would land some glorious leading role, already imagining my name picked out in neon lights, I had religiously learnt my lines. I had practised the movements and gestures in front of a mirror, I had stood there tossing my hair this way and that, I had posed and pouted, practised meaningful gazes; and travelled down to Brighton.

With a ghastly flash of self-awareness I realized how I had tricked myself into the journey, thought myself round the irritation I had felt from his letter. It had been nothing more than a pathetic exercise in self-deception. I had decided that if I travelled down the night before the meeting, did not follow his instructions precisely, then I would be thumbing my nose at his authority and maintaining my control.

Wearily I turned away from the window and began to collect my things together. It was done in a minute. I looked around, trying to think of something else to do, then slumped down on the edge of the bed, leaden, feeling that at any moment I would burst into tears. What could I do? Where could I go? I would simply have to catch the train back to London and resume my old life. The Brighton idea, moving down here permanently, was absurd, this dreary grey place would be even worse than the city: I'd starve in the winter. There was no reason to go back, no reason to stay here, no reason to do anything.

Inexplicably I suddenly thought of Fox and wondered if he ever felt like this. Did he ever question what he was doing? When we'd been back to my flat would he wonder suddenly why he'd done it? That would be the usual way. Afterwards, when they've finished their business they all lie there thinking the same. Why did I come here? Why did it suddenly seem so necessary? You can see it in their eyes – when they're sated or spent their eyes take on a glazed glassy look as if they're perplexed. They are trying to understand how they had felt, how that desire had seemed to be more important than anything else in the world. Fox was sure to be the same. He was probably ugly or the gibbering kind – at this very moment working himself up into a frenzy of excitement, giggling shamefully in anticipation. And yet . . . again . . . that letter . . . it's firmness . . . its decision . . .

I remember exactly what I thought then. I thought, well, you have got to go to the station at some time, why not go there early and take a peek at him? When you've seen what he's like, then you can make the final decision.

I arrived at 11 a.m.: over half an hour before the train I was expected to catch was due to depart. As I walked in under the awnings there was the last announcement for the London train that ran thirty minutes before mine, and for a second I hesitated, considered reversing my decision once more and catching the earlier one instead. I checked my step, felt suspended, unable to choose – until it was finally decided for me. The ticket-collector slammed the gate closed and I watched blankly as the train slid away from the platform and out into the morning; another opportunity I'd either missed or subsconsciously taken.

I seated myself on an odd two-armed bench built around a pillar. It commanded a view of most of the platform gates and was directly in front of the departures board where I was sure he would pause to check. The train I was to take was already standing in the platform; clearly it just shuttled back and forth between London and Brighton, no locomotive to change round. I lit a cigarette and waited.

At first, following the departure of that previous train, there was no one to watch. My eyes wandered, taking in the two great glass-covered awnings that spanned the station, airy and filled with light. A station official sauntered past, then struggled up on to the rostrum below the board and fiddled with the slats. It clicked suddenly and a new list of destinations appeared. He hopped down again and walked off. My eyes darted about nervously, recording all there was to see, examining every new entrant to the station.

After about ten minutes the first few London-bound travellers had gathered at out gate, straggling in an awkward line,

41

uncertain as to whether they were queueing or not. He was not amongst them, but I was not surprised, it was still quite early.

A train came in and a host of new arrivals were spilled on to the platform. They marched determinedly to the gate and swept out, pushing through the growing throng of London travellers who were forced to shuffle into a bunch. Suddenly it became difficult to see everyone; I scanned them all anxiously but was unable to pick out a grey suit.

Five minutes later the gate was opened. The crowd immediately surged forward and then spread out along the platform moving fast as if it were a race of some kind. Still there was no sign of him. 11.20 passed.

Soon people began to stream into the station and I was having trouble keeping up. There were families with children, young men and women, a lot of middle-aged women elegantly dressed, evidently travelling up to town for the day, but few older men.

11.25. He was cutting it fine.

An old man swathed in blankets was wheeled past by a nurse. I stared at him considering whether it could possibly be Fox. He was shrunken and withered, with red rheumy eyes – clearly very sick and I was forced to laugh at myself for having given it so much as a thought. But where was the man?

11.30 now. If I didn't move I would miss the train myself. I felt helpless, hardly able to keep up with the last-minute arrivals, both desperate now to see him and yet hoping that I had missed him: I could not believe that he would arrive this late.

An elderly man with a black greatcoat limped by, leaning on a stick. What about him? A semi-invalid? It was just possible; unlikely, but possible. I followed him through the gate and on to the platform, watching as he heaved himself into the nearest carriage, then stood by it myself. He turned briefly and looked out: it couldn't be Fox, he was seventy-five at least. I swung round rapidly in case I had missed any other possible candidates. There were only two minutes. He must come. The guard was hovering beside me, his whistle at the ready. Where was Fox for God's sake?

And then a new thought. I had got the wrong day. The wrong train. I snatched out my ticket. There was nothing wrong.

A last flurry of travellers. The gate closed.

No Mr Fox. I swore under my breath. The stupid fool had funked it.

Immediately I had climbed on board and slammed the door shut, the train jerked forward. The racing of my heart slowed, but there was no way I could pretend to myself that I was not disappointed. It was too late now, I would never know.

I leant against the door and attempted a sigh of relief, but it was useless. I didn't feel relieved. The whole thing was ridiculous; despite trying to remind myself that he'd paid for my brief holiday, I still felt it had been nothing more than a waste. The script, the rehearsals, the ticket, the agonizing build-up of nerves, just a waste. The platform slipped past apparently gathering speed so that the porters, the benches and the pillars supporting the station whipped by, at last spinning off free like the final frames of a film unhooking from a reel. I was alone, there at the very rear of the train, my dejection deepening, suddenly nothing to look forward to again. And the irony of it. After all my hopeless hesitations, my dithering over the decision, it was he who had chickened out, not I. I felt a rush of anger.

I watched disconsolately through the window as we scuttled free of Brighton, then pulled the ticket from my bag deciding that I might as well have the benefit of the first-class seat since he'd paid for it. It was marked C46, a carriage up near the front of the train. I began working my way forward, bad-temperedly knocking into people as I went.

I never expected him to be there. That is the truth. I was totally convinced that since I had not seen him on the station he could not possibly be on the train. I still don't understand how it was I didn't see him; I can only assume he had travelled down on that very same train and then sat there waiting for it to make its return journey. But as I approached the compartment I felt a tiny renewal of hope – there was this last chance. As soon as I saw him the hope turned to panic.

In a sense it was funny – I had only glanced in – in my confusion of disappointment and anger I overshot the door and only understood what I had glimpsed after I had passed. A grey suit, a full head of completely silver hair, gold-rimmed glasses. He had been sitting in the corner, staring out of the opposite window.

I stood in the corridor about two doors down, shaking. Suddenly I felt my breakfast in my throat, a churning in my stomach. I could not control it. Oh no, I thought, what have you done? You could have sat anywhere, you would not have seen him. There was that other train, those other seats; how did you ever get yourself into this?

Then I crashed against the side. The train was now hurtling into a curve and the sudden lurch had thrown me against the window-rail, bruising my arm. I stood there for a time, clutching the bar, cursing softly both at the sudden pain and my own stupidity. I rubbed the spot, decided to have a cigarette, then changed my mind. I felt quite helpless. I was sure that he hadn't seen me, that I could still sit elsewhere, but somehow I felt that I could not get out of it now, that there was no way of backing down. I had come so far – made the positive decision at so many points along the route – that it was impossible for me to avoid this last one. I would have to go in. An image flashed through my mind: waiting in the wings. And that old trick of children: after ten to make your move.

I started counting. And ended. Now. I forced myself along and slid back the door to the compartment.

It was incredible; there is no other word to describe it. When I walked in he simply looked up – perhaps a bit startled, but no more than anyone would have been by a sudden entrance, said 'Good morning', then resumed his gaze through the window.

I was flabbergasted. My heart was thumping so hard that I was speechless, and I stood there gaping stupidly at him, expecting him to say something like 'Ms Rivers?', and then grin. But he didn't. He didn't seem interested in me in the least, totally denying that he had had anything to do with organizing the whole thing. His eyes had hardly acknowledged me. They had just flickered across me as any traveller's would, momentarily dragged from a reverie. I was another unextraordinary person who had entered his life for the length of a journey. I felt my legs tremble, at that moment aware for the first that I had got myself into something I could not handle, suddenly afraid.

And then I couldn't close the door. I had entered with such a frenzied burst that it had got stuck back, jammed wide open. I struggled with it, feeling the blood rushing to my face. And he simply stood up. A second later his voice came from behind, smooth as butter, unnerving, 'Can I do it for you?' I nodded weakly, squeezed out a 'Thank you', and he slid it closed with hardly an effort.

Still there was no signal of recognition, no sly wink or anything, he simply closed it firmly behind us and the screaming of the rails suddenly died. All went silent. The world was shut out; all sense of reality was left behind. I put my bag up on the rack, took my seat in desperation and watched him return to the window.

He *was* about sixty. At least that was a relief. Secretly, perhaps even trying to hide it from myself, I had been afraid that the letter might have been a trick, that he'd lied about his age to get me unsuspectingly to the carriage and might prove to be one of the violent types. He was ageing – though not aged – an unthreatening man. And it had to be him. I checked the suit again in case the light had deceived me; but it was pale-grey as the letter had promised.

He sat down slowly, threw me an uncomplicated smile and drew his hand through the great mane of silver hair. I had got him completely wrong. There was nothing of the dribbling trouser-stained kind about him: he sat straight-backed, his gold-rimmed glasses carefully adjusted, a bearing in his posture. There was a sort of sad dignity about him – an aura that the old attract around them, the sense that they have lived through times of pain and sorrow that you could not even begin to imagine.

And he was still attractive. The jaw was firmly cut, the nose not puffed or purpled, only the bags under his eyes magnified by the spectacles gave away the years. I felt my gaze drawn down to his hands clasped easily on his lap; the skin was blotched with brown marks like tea-stains, another reminder that he was no longer young. Momentarily I felt a tiny ripple of sadness at the thought of people growing old in this way, decaying slowly, withering like plants. I thought he must have been quite striking as a young man. There was a gold signet ring on his little finger — I wondered idly if he had ever married.

He must have sensed me gawping in this way for he suddenly turned, removed his glasses and looked at me directly. He had enormous soft blue eyes, quite kind really, but he fixed me with such a stare that I had to look away. I began fumbling nervously in my shoulder bag for the book I was supposed to read and opened it at the first page I came to.

I see now that his intention must have been exactly that — to remind me of who I was and what I was meant to be doing, for he did not speak or do anything else, but carefully replaced his glasses and turned away as soon as I had begun to read. Without my realizing, the play had started.

For a time I even made an unsuccessful effort to concentrate on the book. Besides the fact that I had no more than glanced at it previously, and for the purposes of the script was on the point of finishing the book, with Fox sitting only a couple of feet away I could not hope to understand a thing. I flipped through the pages, re-reading sentences innumerable times but taking nothing in; they might as well have been written in a foreign language. I felt him glance at me on a few occasions and when the train rushed through a tunnel he had no choice but to look across for something to occupy his eyes. Each time I became more anxious, increasingly certain that he would speak or make a move. I knew the dialogue was not due to start until after we had stopped at Croydon, but I was sure he would say something, that there would be an explanation of what was going on – or if not that, at the very least some hint of what exactly he was expecting. But there wasn't. He did nothing, said nothing, just continued gazing through the window.

Once, when I shifted my position so that I was holding the book up slightly, I noticed that in the glass giving out on to the corridor I could see his reflection. I pretended to read but watched him closely.

He stretched his legs out, rested his chin on his hand, but otherwise did not move. The thought occurred to me that he might be observing me in exactly the same way and I winked but there was no reaction.

A little later I tried crossing my legs provocatively, letting my skirt ride up above the knees, but he seemed completely involved in the passing scene outside the window. We remained in total silence; an absurd piece of theatre.

The unreal quality of it all was broken only once: when the guard arrived to check our tickets. He burst in so unexpectedly, violently sliding the door back, that I almost dropped the book. The clatter of the rails was suddenly amplified to full volume again, somehow reassuring.

I could not find my ticket but Fox leant across almost immediately and held out his; it was clipped, and then the guard waited while I searched frantically through my bag.

'The others haven't turned up then?' he said.

The question was not directed at either one of us in particular, but for a moment I did not understand. Then I remembered the little 'reserved' tickets pinned to the other seats.

'Evidently not,' said Fox quietly.

The guard shook his head. 'Some bloody people must have money to burn,' he complained, then began snatching the cards from the empty places.

I found my ticket finally, and the guard left without another word. Once again the outside world was cut out, the noise dying the second the door was slammed shut. As soon as he was gone I realized the significance of the tickets he had taken: Fox must have reserved the whole compartment to ensure that we were not disturbed.

After that I could not think straight. Already we had reached Gatwick. We were hurtling along. A plane was coming in to land, sweeping low over the train as we passed. In a matter of minutes we would be at Croydon and the dialogue would start. A blank curtain came down over my brain – I could not remember who spoke first, the opening line. I turned to the last page of the book, scanning it hurriedly as if there I might find a clue. How did it start? God only knows how many times I read the final page of that book. I looked at each word desperately, but nothing went in. I just remember the final sentence – a man asking a woman: 'You will come, won't you?' and leaving you there suspended. It had its significance I see now, but at the time it just made me feel more strange, more disorientated, less able to cope.

Then we were running through the beginnings of the conurbation – there would be no more open countryside, just denser and denser housing, more scrappy and dilapidated the nearer we approached London. I kept telling myself that there was still time to escape – Christ, I could just stand up and walk out of the compartment; get off at Croydon if I wanted – there was no authority to keep me here.

My heart began to quicken; I was hot and breathless, the carriage all of a sudden stuffy. I glanced quickly round the compartment, taking in the neatly arranged lay-out, the blue, buttoned cloth, the starched white head-rests, the reading lamps, the mirror.

Fox was gently tapping his fingers on the ledge below the window.

Through the corridor window I watched as we overtook a van on the road below the embankment: it was a rental company's, based in Croydon.

Then we started the long curve round a growing cluster of houses and the train checked slightly. I heard the brakes grind as they were slowly tightened; a gentle juddering and then a sound like a kettle coming up to the boil. We pulled into the station, jerked to a halt and waited. Time felt suspended.

A couple of doors clicked open, there was shouting along the platform and then dull thuds as the doors were swung shut. I did not look up. I stared frozenly at my book. It was my cue. When the train moved I was to close it, having finished the novel.

I was sure then that I would not be able to do it.

Six

It's odd: whenever I had imagined acting I had thought that the first time one would have to be pushed on stage or be given a kick from the wings. It doesn't happen like that. I can see now that when the moment comes, when you hear your cue ring out you don't say, 'I won't go on', you just get on and do it. You don't have time to think, you're programmed to react instinctively.

The train jerked forwards. I had practised the movement a thousand times: sort of letting the book fall and sighing softly. To my surprise – or horror – I found that I had started.

He glanced across and spoke, his voice friendly, almost amused.

'Did you like it?'

I looked up at him. He was smiling; difficult to describe – wryly and a bit superior.

'I . . . I'm sorry?' I said. My voice came out weak and high.

'The book – I couldn't help noticing – did you enjoy it?'

'Oh! I see what you mean. Yes . . . yes I did; very much. Have you read it?'

He didn't reply immediately and I realized I had gabbled my

lines. I wondered if the pause was to slow me down, but he didn't seem disconcerted.

'Er . . . yes. A number of times actually,' he answered finally.

'Really? Well, you must have liked it.'

He smiled again but did not answer.

'The end was rather frustrating,' I went on quickly.

'Oh yes?'

'You don't know what happens to them . . . I mean, you don't know if they went through with it.'

'No you don't, that's true.'

'It spoils the story – it's as if the author didn't know how to finish it.'

He paused to think about the comment, as if he hadn't considered the point before.

'I suppose it's possible that he didn't,' he said at last.

'You don't sound as if you believe that.'

'Well . . . maybe not.'

There was another silence.

'You don't give much away,' I said.

He grinned, then sat forward as though he had reached some conclusion. 'Did you read the epigraph?'

'Er . . . yes, I think so.'

'It's there.'

'What? The answer?'

'Yes. Could I see the book a moment?'

'Of course.'

He stretched out his hand on cue but could not reach the book (as the script had indicated he wouldn't), so he edged across into the middle seat opposite me. As he took the book I noticed that his hand was shaking minutely and it startled me: it hadn't crossed my mind that he might be nervous as well. I tried to analyse what was happening – we'd followed the script exactly and yet it did not quite feel like a play – more like real life and I was surprised to observe that I had not had to struggle with my lines.

He pushed his glasses up on to his forehead as someone who is short-sighted might, then searched for the page. When he found it he held the book out at arm's length and squinted.

'Here you are,' he said, then began to quote. His voice was almost croaky, each weighed precisely.

'Quick now, here, now, always –
Ridiculous the waste sad time
Stretching before and after.'

He held the book a moment longer, gazing at it silently. His eyes were soft.

'Where's that from?' I asked as scripted.

'Eliot – "Burnt Norton".'

'Oh.'

'Does it make it clear?'

'I'm not sure exactly. You still don't know whether or not they got together.'

He shuffled with a trace of irritation, somehow boyish.

'That's just the point! It doesn't matter if they did or not –—don't you see? You're not meant to know for certain – the author didn't want you to.' He waited for me to say something but I was scripted to keep silent. 'The moral is obvious anyhow.'

'Is it?'

'Of course it is.'

'What then?'

He looked up at me, fixing me with a hard stare so that for the first time I felt uncomfortable.

'All time is unredeemable,' he said slowly. 'There are no second chances.'

He closed the book and looked at it distantly. I nodded, only half-understanding, but went on.

'I see,' I said. 'You mean if they didn't sleep together, they should have.'

'It was their responsibility. Otherwise there was no point to what happened before or after.'

He glanced up at me to see my reaction. Perhaps then, right then, back at the outset of the whole business I should have had the first glimmer of what was going on but it was all so abstruse, so confused, that I couldn't see my way through it. I felt sure he would explain, tell me what it was that he wanted. I hurried on, lightly.

'All the same, it's still frustrating. He has no right to finish a book like that.'

His mood changed. He gave a kind of distant laugh and snorted. 'I agree with you absolutely.'

I watched him for a moment as he looked back at the book again, took in the cover, then handed it across. His eyes caught mine and for the briefest second I thought he'd winked; there was that twinkle in them. I felt confused, no longer certain that he was acting, unsure in myself as to what had just happened. But whatever it was it had passed. He leant back against the seat once more and immediately looked out of the window. There was a break in the script there, a breathing-space, and I too glanced out remembering that he had the next line and would choose when to start. I let myself relax.

We had started to run into Streatham now and the tracks beside us multiplied into a complex of interweaving patterns racing and darting beneath the window. A car dump passed with piles of rotting tyres and layers of rusting, crumpled metal barely resembling vehicles; then a station, the people sitting and standing like plastic miniatures on a model railway.

I wondered idly how I had sounded: whether or not I'd made my lines seem natural. It had been much easier than I had thought it would be – we hadn't deviated from the script at all, but that made it more peculiar still. I was sure that he would have to make his move in a minute.

'Do you live in London?'

He had spoken again – as scripted – but its suddenness and that traveller's politeness caught me unawares and I had to snap myself back into consideration.

'Well . . . sort of,' I replied.

'I'm sorry, it's none of my business.'

'No, no – I didn't mean it like that. It's just that I've been back to visit my family and I can never work out whether there or London is home now.'

'You're a student?'

'Yes.'

'Of what?' He checked himself and gave a half-amused expression. 'I'm sorry, this must sound like an interrogation.'

'No, it's all right, I don't mind,' I said, 'but see if you can guess.'

He threw a hand up to his face. 'Oh my goodness, I asked for that.'

'Go on – have a try.' I tried to sound teasing as the script had directed, realizing that the character I was playing was intended to be less timid than I was seeming.

'All right . . . Art?' he suggested.

'Wrong! Why did you choose art?'

'I don't really know.'

'Oh come on, you must have had a reason. I'll bet it was the clothes.'

'Perhaps,' he said sheepishly. We both laughed as scripted. Mine came out a little hysterically in my nervousness and I saw him wince. I had to keep going.

'Have another try.'

He thought. 'Er . . . Music?

'No.'

'English?'

'No.'

'Oh dear, this is becoming embarrassing.' He grinned. 'How about Nuclear Physics?'

'No!' I laughed again, pleased to hear this time that it sounded more natural.

'Give me a clue.'

The script had then said I was to 'ham it up'. I put on my most actressy voice and recited: ' "Wherefore art thou Romeo?" '

'Drama, of course.'

'At last.'

'How stupid of me – I should have guessed.'

He sank back in his seat and smiled. The whole business seemed to ridiculously harmless that its innocence suddenly threatened me. A twinge of fear prickled my skin – I wondered if things would turn nasty after all. His control was so complete that I looked away to the window in desperation and as soon as I did so a new thought shocked me.

We were gliding through Clapham Junction now, swiftly approaching London, and the sight of the station brought home to me something that I had never before considered. He must have timed it, timed the whole thing. He must have timed the dialogue down to the last second so that it would coincide with our arrival at Victoria. It was the most crazy elaborate arrangement: the tickets, the reserved compartment, the closing of the book – it was all organized down to the tiniest detail. He must have rehearsed it.

What happened next nearly finished me. I forgot my lines. It was the shock of course, that sudden flash of understanding, but my mind went a complete blank and I began to panic. There was a horrible silence. Outside the lines were dividing. Everything was slipping away from me. I could feel the blood rushing to my face.

I should have said then, 'O.K., that's it, I've had enough of all this,' but for some reason that idea terrified me even more; I looked at him helplessly, agonizing for the safety of the script.

'I . . . er . . . ' I began stammering, then said, 'Oh God!'

His smile disappeared immediately and an expression of weary despair crept across his face. I had completely ruined the effect. He waited a moment longer. In the distance I could see Battersea Power Station – we were nearly at Victoria. I prayed to be rescued. If only I could remember my line, if I could just hang on till we got there.

'What about you.' The prompt was whispered, as if an audience might hear. The whole thing flooded back.

'Oh God, yes.' I blurted out, then attempted to recover – the scripted line rushing out in a sudden torrent. 'What about you? And don't ask me to try because I haven't got a clue.'

It sounded absurd, but his frown cleared and he hesitated. I wasn't sure if it was acting or whether I had thrown him as well.

'I . . . I'm at Sussex.' Then quickly, 'I lecture there – as well as on trains.'

I laughed. 'English by any chance?'

'No, no.' He relaxed. 'French.'

'I failed that at school.'

He smiled and shrugged his shoulders.

'But I like to believe that was the teacher,' I said.

'Yes, it usually is our fault, I'm afraid.'

I laughed again, more relieved that I had recovered some composure than amused by the comment. We were passing over the Thames now and we both looked over towards Chelsea Bridge. It gleamed white in the cold sunlight, a bus crossing, brightly red. I felt the end in sight, the tone much easier.

'Anyway acting is far more interesting,' he said. 'Tell me more about that.'

'It's just a job.'

'I'm sure it isn't.'

'It is sometimes, believe me. When you're working at a part.'

The train was slowing and again I heard that sound like water boiling.

'Are you very good?'

'You can't seriously expect me to answer that.'

'Why not?'

'It wouldn't be modest if I said "yes", now would it?'

'Try.'

He was sitting forward on the edge of his seat. I gulped. 'All right,' I said, 'I'm bloody brilliant.'

His eyes twinkled for a moment again, then he sat back.

'I thought perhaps you were,' he said and winked. I was thrown again, not sure any longer which was the reality. Did the wink suggest that I was good, or just this character I was playing? The script had not mentioned a wink.

But the ordeal was almost over. The train had begun edging in along the platform and the sounds of shouting and slamming from outside intruded into the compartment. I had a fleeting sensation of at last returning to sanity, the journey now finished, the script almost at an end.

He stood up suddenly and smoothed down his clothes.

'Well we seem to have arrived,' he said. 'Good luck with the

56

drama anyway – it's a pity, I would have liked to hear more about it.'

'Well, maybe next time I travel up I can tell you.'

He smiled. I put the book in my bag and made to stand up too.

'And thank you for enlightening me about the novel. Which of his do you recommend next?' My legs felt weak as I pulled myself up; the train lurched to a halt and I almost fell back. His hand steadied me.

'Oh, I'm not sure. Maybe *Starting Back*.' He paused, one hand resting on the door handle. 'No, wait. *The Duet* – you'll like that.'

'Why?'

'The ending is very clear – the couple make a suicide pact.'

'Did you have to tell me?'

'Sorry!' He smiled. 'I couldn't resist it.'

He slid the door back and a blast of cold air hit us. I felt suddenly elated knowing that I had virtually made it.

'Can I take your bag for you?'

'It's all right, thanks.'

He waited while I lifted it down, then gestured for me to move into the corridor.

The last few lines were scripted to take place on the platform. He did not say a word until we were there, and for a time I thought once more that he would chicken out, drop the pick-up part altogether. We fell into step towards the barrier, people suddenly all around; an audience. I felt relieved, glad ironically to be back in London now, a territory I knew. I suspected that the game would change – that now we were in real life again things would be different; the secret world of that compartment left behind.

A porter stepped back just as I was passing, causing me to check my step and Fox blundered into me. His reaction was extravagant; he leapt aside as if he had touched a live wire, then apologized clumsily and over-emphatically. Clearly, I realized, we were not meant to touch – at least not yet. There was no pawing at me, no attempt to make use of it as an excuse. We resumed our step.

Finally about ten yards from the barrier he stopped.

'Look, I've got a free half-hour. Do you fancy a drink?' The soft blue eyes were nervous now. 'I know a fairly decent place just around the corner.'

I thought: here we go; put on my Lolita-voice.

'I really ought to get along to the school, I'm afraid. There's a rehearsal this afternoon.' He looked disappointed despite the fact that this was scripted. 'Thanks all the same.'

'Don't misunderstand me. Just a quick drink . . . '

'I'd like to really . . . but . . . '

There was a short silence, people brushing past. He wainted until they had gone, then quoted, questioningly:

' "Quick now, here, now . . . " '

I took it up. ' "Ridiculous the sad waste time" – was that it?'

'Almost – "the waste sad time" – but near enough.'

I laid it on a moment longer, then:

'Well all right then. Why not? Just one though . . . '

'You're on,' he said and grinned.

I gave a sigh of relief. That was the end of the script. He nodded his head. It was as if he was congratulating me on my performance. I felt like saying: 'Was I good? or, 'Aren't you going to applaud?' but I never got the question out – he had started walking again and I was forced to follow.

When we reached the gate not a word was said. We gave up our tickets and began moving away towards the exit.

All of a sudden I felt my mood change. I'm not sure exactly why; I think I must have glanced at him and seen the anxiety betrayed in his face, but whatever it was I felt suddenly depressed. I remembered what was to come. I thought, well, that's it, the holiday's over now, it's back to work again. So much for the fun, the little play-acting game. It had made a change and was quite novel while it lasted, but now the real business of the trip must start. And I simply could not fact it. The scene in the pub, slow dispelling of the whole pretence. In a couple of hours' time we would be back at the flat. I looked at him, saw him as all the others in that aftermath, lying there trying to understand why it was that he had had to do it. I had been an idiot to forget it; now I felt sick and angry. The hollow chill of the station only emphasised the feeling; common, cheap and squalid. I made up my mind to say something.

I'm not quite certain what I would have said – something sarcastic no doubt, like: 'Well, Mr Fox, that was jolly good fun – what happens now then?', but I never said it. I didn't get the chance. I was saved in a sense – I would have broken the golden rule of never asking questions.

We were almost at the exit. He stopped in his tracks and clasped his forehead.

'Oh damn!'

'All right, what is it?' I said.

'I've left my umbrella in the train.' He did not look at me. 'Look, will you hang on here a moment while I pop back and get it?'

'Sure,' I said. I shrugged my shoulders. 'Whatever you say.'

'I won't be more than a couple of seconds.'

I nodded disinterestedly and he turned and went. I watched as he marched purposefully back to the barrier. His silver hair bobbed up and down as he walked, then I lost sight of him in the crowd.

I stood there gazing blankly at the bustle of people, wondering what to do. He had given me the chance to make my escape if I wanted – now was the time to give him the slip, the moment I had decided earlier at which I could always back out. Now it was here I didn't know what I wanted. I tried to picture him, but already his face had gone. Yet he hadn't tried to rape me, he hadn't tried anything on. I looked around, the tired faces of boredom, the empty voices echoing around the station. There was nothing, simply nothing to which I could look forward. My holiday in Brighton was over, the acting was done. I didn't want to stay, yet I couldn't make myself go. If I waited, what would happen? Maybe I *had* got him wrong. The quotation I'd learnt came back for no reason. There are no second chances. I shifted my weight to the other foot and put my bag down. I would see what happened at the pub, then make the final decision. But he never returned.

59

Seven

I must have waited for at least twenty minutes before giving up
hope that he would come. At first I pretended that I didn't
mind. Going back on the Underground I made a vain effort to
convince myself that what I felt was not disappointment or
depression but just a silly sense of anti-climax. I told myself that
I should be grateful for what had happened; indeed, I tried to
think myself into being pleased that he had disappeared: I had
not had to suffer the pub-scene, the squalid affair at the flat. At
the last moment he had got cold feet and had pulled out – I had
been spared the sordid part. No, the only reason I felt a bit
down was because I had got it all out of proportion in the first
place; well, I had got my just deserts. I caught sight of my
reflection in the tube-train window and saw an idiot staring
back – innocent, gullible eyes, a silly tart who'd forgotten just
what she was. High-class callgirl! Jane Fonda-like! Such a
brilliant actress I'd even fooled myself.

Another feeling grew, vague at first, just the faintest prick. I
was a tiny bit hurt. He had not found me attractive, he had not
desired me at all. The picture I'd sent him had lied; my eyes did

not smoulder in the least; that was just ridiculous. It had been a trick of the camera, an effect of the light.

Suddenly it swelled out of all proportion. I felt the stare of the other passengers on me, my smock clammy, sticking to my back. The self-confidence I had so precariously constructed suddenly crumbled away around me. London was the worst, the most impersonal place. I felt like a piece of flesh on a butcher's slab, a piece of meat some fussy customer had pointed at then rejected for another. An old man opposite me hawked loudly and lengthily and spat into his handkerchief. I thought I was going to be sick.

That afternoon when I got home, by the most cynical twist of fate, I found the flat had been broken into. They didn't find any money but they took the TV and the radio and smashed a few ornaments just for the hell of it. There was that ghastly atmosphere in the place: that someone has been inside and been looking at all your things, holding your possessions, invading. I felt that I had been violated, obscurely raped. I did not cry. I almost did; but I bought a bottle of vodka and got morosely drunk that night. I remember sitting in an armchair in the silence of the wrecked place blearily waving Fox's cheque in front of my eyes and trying to see the funny side. Pay Ms Sylvia Rivers – that was the last laugh. I couldn't even use it – the final twist of the knife.

It was only when Tom handed me the second envelope a fortnight later that I realized the Brighton trip had only been an audition.

I could not believe it at first. This time I did not bother to take it down to the lavatories to sneak a look at it, but ripped it open straightaway in the office without thinking about whether the others would notice. I remember I did not pull the contents out immediately, but sort of peered inside as though I was afraid of what I might find. There was another wad of paper and a cheque again, loose. I pulled it out. It was for £150. I was completely taken by surprise.

I must have gone absolutely white – June, one of the other typists, was watching me and she asked me what was wrong. It so flustered me that I stuffed the cheque back into the envelope, not knowing what to reply and giving the game away completely. She asked me again if I was all right. I racked my brains for something to say, but nothing would come. Then she said I was looking pale. She offered to get me a drink and began to get up. An answer came from somewhere, some recess of my mind – the only thing I could think of. I said spluttering that it was all right, there was nothing wrong – it was just that my father had sent me some money, that was all. She clearly didn't believe me. She threw me a disapproving look, prepared to say something, then thought better of it. I began sorting through some papers on my desk and slipped the envelope into my bag.

I waited half an hour, then succumbed again to temptation. Once again, safely locked in one of the cubicles, fingers trembling with excitement, I tipped out the contents of the envelope.

Again I examined the cheque. No mistake – £150, payable to Ms Sylvia Rivers, and drawn on the same bank: one in central London. I replaced it carefully: between two fingers, like a sliver of glass.

Next, another script. This time it was longer, about five pages, and I skimmed through it. It made no sense again; I decided to examine it more carefully at home.

And then, just as before, there was a letter. No heading. No address. Straight in:

Dear Ms Rivers,
    I was very impressed by your performance on the train on March 21st and must apologize for my unexplained departure.
    I would now be most grateful if you would undertake a further assignment, slightly longer but fairly straightforward. I enclose the dialogue which I would ask you to learn.
    You are to play the same character as you did on the train; the girl's name is Juliet Kent and she is as you know a drama student at RADA. On this occasion you

meet at the Tate Gallery – quite by accident – you have not seen the man since the train journey and drink in the pub. He will be sitting on one of the bench seats opposite a painting entitled 'After Lunch' by Patrick Caulfield in the section on Modern British Painting, at 3.15 on April 11th. Should this date be inconvenient, please contact Box 14 as soon as possible.

Please follow the instructions given in the dialogue precisely, and may I remind you once more not to ask questions. Do not step out of your role in any way.

Once again I enclose a cheque which I hope you will consider adequate for your services. If this is not sufficient write to Box 14 and we will try to come to some arrangement.

I look forward to meeting you on April 11th.

Yours,
P. Fox

It didn't take me long to decide that I would do it. I made up my mind right away, without even having read the script properly. Above all, I was overjoyed that I had not been rejected, I felt all the energy and interest that I had lost over the previous fortnight come flooding back in a tidal wave of sudden confidence: I had landed the part – he had been 'very impressed' by my performance.

When I got home that afternoon I settled down to read the script. To be frank, I can only say that I was disappointed. There was nothing more to learn about him there – I had hoped for an explanation of the whole thing within the dialogue but there wasn't one at all. It was more intellectual still, artier even than the dialogue on the train and yet more perplexing. There were not even any more details about who he was exactly, there was no information about where he came from, where he lived – the only thing that was revealed was his first name: Paul. At least that fitted – P. Fox, Paul Fox – but it did not help me in any way.

What was really extraordinary was the way the set-up had changed. I'd thought the first dialogue was a pick-up; an old man about to proposition a girl; in this the situation was reversed. I was to proposition him. He'd somehow made me the instigator of the whole arrangement; I wondered vaguely if this had been his aim from the very outset – to make him feel he was being chosen by me rather than the other way around. Obscurely I thought this might be some kind of way of avoiding a moral problem: did he feel that by making the girl the forward one he would not be responsible for what happened?

For indeed the girl, Juliet, was forward. That directness and self-confidence that I'd noticed in her character in the first script was there again, and more pronounced – she teased, almost cajoled him along. She was forthright, lively and quite amusing; I found myself feeling jealous: I thought I wouldn't mind being more like her – the Fonda-thing again no doubt. To my surprise I realized that I had begun to look forward to playing the part.

Of course by the time April 11th came I was reduced to a nervous wreck. Admittedly it was only just over a week since I had received the script, but I had spent every free moment working at it, trying to get it absolutely right.

According to the script I was to have a copy of the Gallery guide in my hand so I'd been down to the Tate already and bought one and taken the opportunity at the same time to check where all the paintings the script referred to were – in all I'd really worked hard at the part and taken it very seriously.

I'd also opened a new bank-account. From what I'd gathered from the ending of this script I was sure there'd be another one and if I coped with this one all right, then surely there'd be another cheque. I was eager to get on, keen to get this business at the Gallery over with so we could start work on the next. Only very occasionally did my previous fears come back to haunt me – I no longer seriously considered that he was one of the sad, pathetic types – I'd almost forgotten in fact what our relationship really was.

I waited outside the Tate from 2.30 onwards. I dressed more or less in the same way as I had done for the train – striped

T-shirt, jeans and boots this time, but still very much the drama student part. Today however it was a colder windier day and I put on a shiny metallic-look ski jacket which I decided would be appropriate to the image. I went three-quarters of an hour early to sneak a look at him again – off-stage as it were. I'm not quite sure what I imagined I might see that would help me to understand the situation – the direction he came from? A car? A companion? – in any case it was time wasted for I learnt nothing more. A group of ageing hippies had draped themselves over the white flight of steps leading up the main entrance and I hid myself behind them hoping Fox would not see me when he arrived. He didn't. At 3 p.m., so that he had fifteen minutes in which to position himself, a taxi drew up outside the gates and Fox stepped out. He looked exactly the same as on the previous occasion: the silver hair, the glasses, the grey suit, but this time he was wearing a heavy overcoat, expensive-looking, a Burberry perhaps.

In a way I'd expected him to look furtive; I'd envisaged him glancing round nervously to see if he was being followed – the whole secret thing. But he didn't at all. He paid off the taxi-driver, glanced at his watch and then marched straight into the building, looking neither to the left nor the right, just straight ahead: a man who had some business inside. I was a little disappointed, I half-wanted to see his reaction on seeing me before the appointed time – would he acknowledge me or look away? – I guessed the latter or the script would have made little sense. In any case I was not to know, for he disappeared inside the ponderous darkness of the building almost as quickly as he arrived.

I sat there for a few minutes longer then picked myself up and strolled inside. A sudden fear filled me when I saw all the people milling about: this time the performance would not be in the secluded world of the compartment, there would be people all around us, maybe blocking our view of the pictures we were meant to examine, bumping into us, interrpting even. Suddenly I felt that I would be unable to cope, daunted by the thought of what lay ahead. Again the idea of backing out began to tease at me – I'd got his money, I didn't have to be there, anyone else in their right mind would be out at this very moment spending the hundred he'd sent, not making a fool of herself in the Tate.

I was almost on the point of turning to go when I suddenly thought, no, this is wrong – it's the goose and the golden egg. There's more to come; you can back out when he's sent the next script and the money. Fifteen minutes and it will all be over. Besides, if you're absolutely honest, you would quite like to know what happens.

Eight

He was sitting exactly where he said he would be, on the bench seat opposite the painting he'd mentioned. I could not see his face as I approached – I was not intended to – the meeting was to be a surprise. I could picture the scene. He was meant to be having a short rest; he had been in the Gallery for about an hour and was tired of standing, now he was having a five-minute sit-down before continuing. I moved up so that I was only about five yards behind him, aware, for the first time, that I held some power.

The painting was weird, a little unsettling. It showed the inside of a restaurant, a table, some chairs, a partition, the signs of a room behind, and a figure leaning over a hatch or saloon-door. On the partition there was a poster of an Alpine lake and castle; in front of that, an aquarium with a few fish swimming. Nothing out of the ordinary, it was all perfectly believable: the scene inside a quiet Italian restaurant perhaps. What was odd was the way in which it had been painted: the whole scene was done in blue-print only; the tables, the chairs, even the figure, were only shapes that had been filled out – with the exception of

67

the Alpine picture. This last had been done in minute detail, like an enormous photograph: it was super-real, for even the blue haze of the mountains was perfectly reproduced. It created a peculiar sensation: it made you question the reality of each – was the poster real or the restaurant or both? Momentarily, as I approached Fox, I had a glimpse of our situation too: who was it here – was it Juliet or merely myself?

I moved up beside the bench and paused, pretending to check whether it was him or not, then leaned forward. He half-turned, sensing a presence, someone near.

'Well, do you like it?' I said lightly, a tease in my voice.

He swung round sharply, looked up startled and then spoke.

'My God! Hello there! What are you doing here?'

'The same as you I should imagine,' I said, 'looking at pictures.'

He smiled. 'I'm sorry, that was a pretty stupid thing to say – you surprised me.'

'I meant to. You looked a world away.' I pointed to the space on the seat beside him. 'May I?'

'Of course.'

I sat down. Thankfully there was no one else on the seats. 'Anyway,' I went on, 'do you like it?'

He looked puzzled. I pointed.

'The picture – do you like it?'

'Oh! Yes, I do. How about you?'

'I think we've been here already.'

'Eh?'

'The book, don't you remember? On the train that was the first thing you said to me: "Did you like it?"'

He laughed. I noticed his eyes again; they twinkled with that peculiar amusement: inner, not really for me. 'So I did, you're quite right.' He paused, then, 'Well, it's my turn now – what's your verdict?'

I put on a serious attitude, posing, a hand outstretched.

'I think the picture within a picture element heightens the sense of the surreal, don't you?'

He turned to look at me, affecting an expression of surprise.

'If it hadn't been you that had said that, I would have believed it was from a guide-book.'

I giggled. 'It is. I've just read it here.' I held up the Gallery guide I'd brought.

He snorted, then we both laughed.

'Yes, I should have remembered you were an actress. I don't think I can match you there.'

The script directions then said I was to show disbelief. I did a kind of double-take and caught his eye. 'Pull the other one, Sam,' I said. It felt odd: the situation too ambiguous for these words. 'Incidentally, what is your name?' I went on, 'You never did tell me at the pub that time.'

'Oh . . . Paul.'

I laughed again, as scripted.

'What's so funny?'

'Oh . . . nothing,' I answered. He was pretending to look hurt.

'Come on – what's wrong with Paul?'

'Nothing. Nothing at all.'

'What is it then?'

'Oh, I don't know . . . you just don't look like a Paul.'

'What name would suit me then?'

'Oh Christ!' I exclaimed. 'I shouldn't have started this . . . a Malcolm or John . . . I don't know . . . Lawrence, Matthew . . . something like that.'

He looked at me oddly. 'I'm sorry, I'll have it changed.'

I sat back, resting on my elbows. 'I'm only teasing you – Paul's a nice enough name.'

'Thank you. I breathe again.'

I was meant to pause there. I waited; clearly the two of them were supposed to have run out of things to say to one another, this chance meeting becoming almost an embarrassment for a moment. I left it a second or two longer, then resumed brightly.

'Well . . . come on.'

He looked blank.

'You're supposed to ask me something.'

'I'm sorry?'

'My name – you're supposed to ask me mine.'

'Oh, sorry!' He feigned relief. 'Well, mademoiselle, could I be so bold as to ask you to furnish me with your name?' He winked.

'You may, sir,' I said grandly. Then quickly, 'I though you'd never ask. It's Juliet. Does it fit?'

'Er . . . yes, I think so. I'm pleased to meet you, Juliet.'

'And I you, sir.'

We shook hands with mock formality and then fell silent once more. The whole affair was even stranger now it was being played – rehearsing I had not realized how many double entendres there were; the play on names, on acting – suddenly it all seemed contrived: for my benefit, not his. I was completely lost.

A couple moved in front of us and began discussing the picture in low whispers. Fox glanced up at them and then down at his hands. After a moment he went on.

'Well, how did the rehearsal go?'

'Which rehearsal?'

'The one you had to rush off to from the pub.'

'Oh fine . . . it's coming along.'

He looked round at me again. 'Shouldn't you be at the Academy now?'

I shrugged. 'Probably. It's nice to get away though. You get so wound up and tense – I often come here to relax. I do a different room each time. I'm up to Dada and Surrealism today.'

'You're in the wrong room then.' He glanced quickly round. 'I thought this was Modern British or something.'

'It is. I followed you in here – you walked right past me. I've been following you for ages trying to make up my mind whether to say hello or not.'

'You made the right decision.'

I turned to him to see his expression but he was looking down at his hands again, as if embarrassed at what he'd just said, that betrayal of feeling. There was another brief silence, then,

'Well, if today's your Surrealist day, perhaps we'd better head along there.'

'It doesn't matter,' I said.

'No, we must.'

'You don't have to come.'

'No, I'd like to.' He grinned. 'You can explain them to me.'

'Jesus!' I said. 'Thank God I've brought my guide-book.'

We both got up simultaneously and for a second I was not sure who was to lead whom. The script had not mentioned anything of this sort but I decided on the spur of the moment that if I was supposed to be the regular visitor then it was more likely that I would do the leading. It was just as well I had been to the Gallery before or we would both have been wandering about for ages. He fell into step beside me and we sauntered out, glancing at the paintings as we went, but not stopping.

I turned to him. 'What are you doing here anyway? It's not such a stupid question really.'

'Oh . . . just killing time,' he said casually. 'I've got to meet my — ' he checked himself as the script had suggested he would — ' that is, I've got a meeting in an hour's time. I thought I'd look in here for a while for something to do. You're right, it is relaxing.'

'What's your meeting?'

'Oh . . . just something to do with the university. Er . . . student enrolments, that sort of thing. Not very interesting.'

As instructed I let the matter drop.

Once again I noted how exactly the thing must have been timed — the period taken up by this section of the dialogue was precisely that needed for the walk through into the section on Surrealist art. Almost immediately the subject was finished we came up face to face with the first exhibit mentioned.

'Right,' he said, then leant closer adjusting his glasses. 'My goodness, what on earth is it?'

The exhibit was a vast glass panel standing in a metal frame; two panels in fact with strange, Heath-Robinson-like machine-designs incorporated in the glass. I had not been able to make head or tail of the thing when I'd first seen it; nor could I now understand it any better.

71

I sa'Oh, you'll like this one.'

'Why?'

'Take a look at the title.'

He leant forward once more and read, then slowly turned his face, beaming with what I could only take to be absolutely genuine amusement. If he was acting – and I could only assume he was since he'd sent the script – then he'd caught the expression perfectly.

'Good Lord!' he said and turned back to read out the name. ' "The Bride stripped bare by her Bachelors, even." You could have fooled me.' He stood upright again, folded his arms and turned to me once more. 'All right, what have you got to say about this one then?'

'Hang on a second.' I pretended to flick through the guide until I found the entry. 'I think I need some inspiration.' I fingered the page, then at last exclaimed: 'Oh wow! You'll really love this. It says here, "Various notes made by the artist and collected together and published under the title *The Green Box* provide a key to this work, which can be interpreted as a diagram of a lovemaking machine. Its ironic and erotic character is reinforced by the depiction of humans as fantastic machines . . . "'

'Yes, well . . . ' he said disparagingly.

'Philistine!'

He had moved away already, over to another painting, this time a mustardy-yellow depiction of two melting twisted figures devouring one another on a chest-of-drawers.

'What's this one?' he said.

'Which? – oh the Dali. He bores me; it's supposed to be about the Spanish Civil War, I think – you know, eating one another and so on. I prefer Magritte.'

'Are there any of his here?'

'Yes, there's one. Over here.' I lead him to the opposite wall and up in front of another picture. It was disturbing: a timeless, morbid vision – in the upper part there was a man asleep, apparently enclosed in some coffin-like box, while in the lower part there was a concrete-like slab in a leaden sky and strange images imprinted in the slab – a candle, a bird, a mirror, a hat, a tie and an apple. I could not understand it in the least but it filled me with distaste, there was a nightmarish quality about it. 'It's called "The Reckless Sleeper",' I said. 'Do you like it?'

He did not answer, but asked another question instead. 'What does the book say about it?'

'Hold on.' I fumbled for the page again and scanned it. 'Well not much really – just that it's Freudian.' He nodded and I went on. 'I prefer some of his others much more. Do you know those ones with the broken windows where the fragments on the floor are pieces of the view outside? I've got a poster of one of those in my flat. You're never quite sure what is real and what is not.'

The second I'd said it I remembered that that was what the very first painting had made me think of and how it unsettled me about the script. Again, but more forcibly this time, I was confused about what was happening – for a time, I'd almost forgotten that I was acting.

'Yes, I've seen them,' he said.

I had to snap back into concentration again.

'And the one of the pipe?' I said.

'What's that?' He turned to me, seriously again, the blue eyes questioning.

'You must have seen it – it's just a painting of this enormous pipe so real that you could almost touch it and it says beneath in big letters: "This is not a pipe". It's great.'

'What is it then if it isn't a pipe?'

'A picture – you know, paint on canvas. It's not a pipe at all.'

He gave that snort again, the way he often did when amused.

'Yes, I get your meaning.' He added: 'A rather dirty trick.'

'Ah . . . that's why I like him,' I said. The script had said 'teasing', but when I said it it came out too heavy, overplayed, and I saw him wince faintly as he had done on occasions in the train. I pressed on. 'By the way, that reminds me, talking of dirty tricks I've got a bone to pick with you.'

He looked a little startled. 'Why, what have I done?'

'That book you recommended.'

He smiled. '*The Duet*?'

'Yes. I've just read it. You told me they both committed suicide at the end, you liar. They emigrated to Australia!'

His mouth twitched with amusement. 'It must have been wishful thinking on my part.'

'Eh?'

'I was so sick of the two of them by the end I was beginning to wish they would shoot one another.'

I looked at him a little perplexed, as scripted, though was unsure of why this was required. I went on.

'It was a rotten trick to play, all the same,' I said.

'Really?' he added casually. 'Besides, I didn't want to spoil the end for you.'

'But you had me thinking all along that they were going to slit each other's wrists or something foul. You are a swine.'

He smirked. 'Ah, that's the art of fiction, isn't it?'

'What?'

'Deception.'

I caught his eye again. He held my gaze only for an instant, then looked away. The whole game was changing with every second; now I was no longer sure that it was I who was teasing, I sensed he was in absolute control and that nothing I could do would alter it.

I had to go on. 'Do you fancy a coffee?' I said brightly, changing the mood once more. 'I'm sick of looking at pictures.'

He hesitated.

'Come on, it's my turn,' I said. 'You bought the drinks at the pub that time.'

He glanced at his watch, puckered his forehead. 'Well, I'd like to really, but – '

'Oh here we go again. That's what I said last time,' I protested.

He smiled. 'Yes you did, I remember. But the difference is that you did have the time on that occasion and this time I don't. I really must get to my meeting. I'm already late.'

'Honestly?'

'Honestly.' He seemed genuine.

I was not looking forward to the next part. I took a breath.

'That's a pity,' I said quietly.

He frowned minutely, as if he had not expected this, then looked at me for a moment. At last he replied, slowly: 'Yes it is.'

There was a silence.

He went on lightly. 'Well, maybe next time we meet I'll let you buy me one.'

'Yes,' I said flatly.

Another silence.

'Well, I'd better be getting along,' he said. His voice attempted cheeriness.

'Yes.'

'What an extraordinary coincidence bumping into you here.'

'Yes it was, wasn't it.'

He paused again not knowing now how to make his exit.

I swallowed, prepared myself for the plunge.

'When's next time?' I said suddenly.

His mouth fell open.

'When are we going to meet next time?'

He was completely speechless. Suddenly I was no longer sure that it had been scripted. I took a deep breath.

'Oh Christ!' I said. 'Look, we're not going to meet again unless we arrange it. Yes, I'm asking you if you would like to see me again. I know I'm a woman and this is strictly against the rules of the game, but there you are, I've said it. These are liberated times.' I paused momentarily. 'I just thought I detected a sense of . . . '

'Regret?'

'Yes.'

He paused once more.

'You did,' he said at last.

I breathed again. Relief.

'Well then?'

He had another crisis of doubt. 'I am at least twice your age you know.'

'So what?'

A silence again. He seemed to be considering the possibilities – not the practicalities – but whether it was possible to,

75

say no, some excuse for backing down. I was not sure all of a sudden that he would go through with it.

At last he nodded, expelling the air between his teeth with a low whistle. 'Well, can I call you next time I'm up in town?'

'All right," I answered slowly. I held his eyes. They were soft, almost helpless. 'You'll have to ring RADA though, I haven't got a phone at home.'

'O.K.' He nodded again. 'Who do I ask for?'

'Juliet Kent.'

'That's all?'

'That'll find me.'

He was embarassed. A group of American-looking tourists was passing by in front and stared round at us so unflinchingly that I was made to feel like an exhibit. Suddenly I remembered that there must have been these people all around throughout the dialogue – I had concentrated so hard that I had been almost totally unaware of them. Now I felt as though I was slowly surfacing, swimming my way back to reality after a long dive. I sensed it in Fox as well, though we still continued with the script.

'Well I'm not quite sure what to say,' he said.

'Don't say anything.'

The American foursome were whispering together, one nodding his head in our direction.

'Look, if you've got to get to your meeting, you'd better go.'

He pulled himself together. 'Yes.'

'And I'm going for a coffee.'

'Right.'

A moment passed.

'So long then.'

'So long.' He nodded.

I paused, looked at him a second longer, then turned and began to walk away. I was extraordinarily conscious of being on stage then: the Americans observing the little vignette they had blundered upon with glee. I felt a swing in my walk that I could not help: stagey, more pronounced than my usual step. I reach the doorway, an open entrance, then swivelled round.

'You will ring, won't you?' I asked as quietly as I could.

He looked across at me a moment, his silver hair gleaming in a stray beam of light, and winked.

I turned again and walked straight out.

Nine

Funnily enough, I did go for a cup of coffee. After leaving Fox I walked straight down to the coffee-bar in the basement of the building and smoked three cigarettes in quick succession.

I knew he would not follow me down; I understood that much about the set-up even then: if that was the end of the script, then I would not see him; and in fact I was glad to be alone. I felt so wound up, so tightly spring by the end of the performance that I could not relax – a thousand questions raced through my mind all competing for attention. Had I performed all right? Would he contact me again? How soon? What had he meant by that wink? Why had I fluffed the line about the dirty tricks?

I think even at that point, all that way back then at the Tate, I was beginning to take a pride in my work. I suppose, from hindsight, you could say until the scripts started coming I had not had anything to really take a pride in; now after this startling performance I felt I could do anything, I would take the world by storm. That afternoon I treated myself to a rather alcoholic lunch.

The next few days dragged by. I was convinced that he would send me another script, but it was at the same time hopelessly frustrating. I couldn't do anything to speed him up and I couldn't see him. He came from nowhere and vanished into nowhere and all I could do was wait.

When I consider it now, the extraordinary thing is how quickly I gave up trying to work out his reason for the whole elaborate scheme – I gave it no thought at all – I became totally bound up in my little acting world. At that time I don't think I would have cared in the least had he told me – I was getting my kick out of it, it was working as some sort of therapy. It seemed to have been designed entirely for my benefit.

I grew more impatient as the days went by; every morning I pestered Tom so that after a while even he began to weary of it and doubt what I was up to. 'Perhaps you ought to tell the poor bloke,' he said referring to the story I had fobbed him off with the first time. I was keen to get my new script, eager to hear what he had to say of the Tate meeting – I wanted to read my 'notices', I suppose.

It finally came about ten days later – the same as before – a brown manilla envelope, but thicker this time. Somehow, and I still don't understand how I did it, I managed to resist the temptation of opening it before I got home.

When I did, the first thing I pulled out was the letter – clearly good reviews had replaced money in order of importance by then. It was the same as before – unheaded, no address, the usual undated abrupt beginning.

Dear Ms Rivers,

Congratulations. Your performance at the Tate was magnificent and exactly what I had desired.

I now feel confident that you will be able to undertake a considerably more demanding assignment – if you are agreeable – and once again I would be grateful if you would learn the enclosed script.

The situation is as follows: Paul has contacted Juliet at RADA and they have arranged to meet. Paul's next trip up to London coincides with a performance of the play in which Juliet is taking part, so they have arranged to go out to dinner at a restaurant after the performance. Paul has been to see the play, is very impressed, and Juliet herself is glittering and elated after her success. They meet in the bar of the restaurant – Paul has gone on ahead and Juliet joins him there.

Please come to Antonio's on Wardour Street at 11.15 p.m. on May 6th. I realize this is very short notice considering the size of the undertaking, but nevertheless I hope it will still be possible. Would you please wear a white calico dress (mid-70s style) and if possible a shoulder-length hair-piece.

Once again I enclose a cheque which I hope you will consider adequate for your services. The usual arrangements apply if this is not so.

I look forward to seeing you on May 6th.

Yours,
Paul Fox

I took out the script. It was much, much longer – the size of a full-length play. I looked straight to the end and smiled slowly as I read the last dozen lines or so. I felt slightly cheated. Then I pulled out the cheque. This time I really was flabbergasted. I had never dreamt of so much. He was totally crazy – the fee went up and up. I stared at it in disbelief. The cheque was now for £300.

That evening I read through the script. It was a peculiar sensation. As the dialogue progressed I found myself drawn in more and more so that by the end I was totally absorbed in their story. The characters seemed to have come to life suddenly, developed their personalities even further so that they were leading an existence outside the script as well – one I could easily visualize, that seemed believable. It was oddly frustrating: when they had been mere mouthpieces of dialogue I had somehow felt I was in control; now I found I had to take a secondary role. I could (and did) urge them on – I willed them to get together, but they did so at their own pace, not at all at the pace I wanted. I was mildly disappointed I think – I wanted them to fall in love – I quite fancied the idea of acting this – but they were so restrained, and he so nervous.

Nevertheless, the script was about falling in love, that much was obvious. The plot of the dialogue was really very straightforward: it merely followed the events of a classically romantic, almost magical evening. Paul and Juliet met in the bar that Fox had referred to in the letter, and from the outset it was destined to go right.

As Fox had said, Juliet was glittering. She was on a high; the play had gone magnificently. When she arrived at the bar she was bubbling over almost unable to contain her excitement. Fox was overwhelmed – he had joked on the train that she was a brilliant actress – but clearly she had been shocked to find this was indeed the case. From such a beginning it was inevitable that some love should blossom. Juliet was so full of love of life that night that she could have fallen for anyone, she swooned; and Paul's occasional stand-offishness was dissipated immediately; the two of them succumbed to the setting: wine and candlelight, soft murmuring, the intimacy of an evening.

What they talked about was not of any special consequence. The subjects ranged over acting, his life, her future – they covered everything. But what they said was not important; it simply drew them nearer one another in mood and prepared you for the endinf the evening.

After the meal he took her home. I was sure that it had to end with them sleeping together, everything seemed right for this, it would have been natural, but to my surprise – and as I've mentioned, disappointment – they didn't, at least, since this was where the script finished, I had to assume that they didn't. They whispered to one another, she snuggled sleepily against him in the taxi, they kissed – but no more; it was sweet and harmless, indeed almost innocuously romantic. For a time I wondered whether this was not true to character – I felt that Juliet would not have waited; she'd forced the issue in the previous script – but she did wait, they would arrange another 'date', and I would have to as well. I felt a strange twinge of jealousy; the idea of this love-scene had its appeal and acting it would be quite demanding, but it would be second-hand, a used version of a love-scene and not the real thing. I was not sure whether I would enjoy the experience.

However, the script did reveal more of Fox. Juliet learnt about him as I did, and this time she questioned him in rather greater detail – she wanted to know everything about him she said. He seemed rather reluctant at first to talk about himself but she kept at him and finally he was forced to relate his life-story.

It was only a potted version, briefly and baldly told. He gave the bare facts and only expanded on them when questioned.

He'd been born and brought up in Leeds, the son of a dentist; good middle-class stock, he said. Certainly I'd detected no trace of a Yorkshire accent and Juliet mentioned the same – what little he'd ever had he'd lost a long time earlier he said – he'd lived in the south almost exclusively from the age of eighteen.

He'd down well at school, shown an aptitude for languages and won a scholarship to Cambridge. University had had to wait however; it was wartime – he was called up, served in the Navy but managed to emerge virtually unscathed, having broken his leg in training and been consigned to a desk job. After the war, in 1946, he'd gone up to Cambridge, taken a first in French and then spent a couple of years in France. Almost as soon as he returned to England he had met Mary, married her in 1952 and started to teach in Bristol.

Juliet asked him about the marriage – though it was clear from the script that she had already asked him something on the subject in the pub after the trip to Brighton. This time he was filling in the details.

He'd been happily married: Mary had been a quiet woman, studying librarianship when he'd met her – but their first child was born a couple of years after they'd married so she'd given it up and never worked again. There were two children in fact – Andrew and Sally, now twenty and eighteen, both studying at college. Then in 1970 Mary had been killed in a car crash. The script told the story without much hint of emotion: she'd been alone, returning from a shopping-trip, hit side-on by a lorry that had failed to stop at a junction.

Juliet did not pursue the matter. She did ask him if he'd ever considered remarrying, and he answered that a couple of years previously there had been someone but it had been a mistake – he realized at the last minute that he'd only really considered it for the sake of the children: to give them a mother. It would not have worked he said, and he had decided to stay single.

He'd moved to Brighton only recently. Now that the children had left home he felt he would like to go somewhere new: he had bought a house on the edge of the Downs and spent most of his time on his only real passion, photography. He led a very quiet life he said, walking a little, and developing his own prints in the darkroom. He read a lot as well, but rarely ventured out to concerts or the theatre – Juliet's play was therst he had seen for about two years.

Juliet asked him about his job, but he didn't say much – it was mostly language work, he said; he had done some translations in the past – of Camus and Aragon – but he didn't bother with that side much now. He was on various university committees which frequently brought him to London, otherwise he stayed at home – he kept away from the university except for his work.

It all seemed reasonable. I recalled that first sight I'd had of him on the train, and the feeling I'd had about him then: that aura of dignity, the sense of a sadness that has been lived through. I could imagine him pottering about on his own; walking, taking photographs; I could imagine that he had lost his wife, that he had two adult children, I could well believe that he described Mary's death in a plain factual way to protect himself – as a kind of safety reaction.

But there was something wrong. I could not work it out at first – I suppose that the truth is, I didn't really bother that much then, but then two things faintly worried me. The first was, what did Juliet see in the man? There was an odd mysterious quality about the man on the train, but when he described himself so mundanely in this script it seemed that there was nothing that would attract a girl like Juliet. I suspected that he was rather under-selling himself of course, but at the same time there had to be something else to make him appeal to someone of Juliet's age – unless it was simply the older-man syndrome.

The other thing that did not quite feel right, that seemed out of character somehow, was this man sending me the scripts, devising these extraordinary games we were playing. I wondered, with a hint of apprehension, if the death of his wife had unhinged him after all, turned him schizophrenic. It was possible I supposed. All clients have problems and we are therapists of a sort, so in a sense there would be nothing unusual in that. They all lead double lives. But to be honest I did not give it a great deal of thought. Perhaps I should have done. Even then I think I'd been given enough clues. I could have checked up on him, I could have made further inquiries then. But I had my own problem as well: I didn't want to destroy any illusion, I was happy enough the way it was. I made a point of overlooking the inconsistencies.

There was one other thing I could have done. I could have written to Box 14 to see how much money I could squeeze him for. When I look at his letter now it is plain that I could have upped my fee without any trouble – he was eating out of my hand even then though I had no idea of it at the time. But I didn't write, I didn't try. I was simply terrified of losing him. I thought, if you try to take him for every penny he's got he might decide to drop the whole scheme, so I left it. Besides, £300 was more than I often made in a month and I never enjoyed playing the game very tough. I put the cheque in the bank and decided not to spend it until I'd actually earned it. In that respect I'd quite a surprise in store.

I enjoyed the preparations for the big night, although this time it was much more difficult learning the script. Being so much longer and with so much more to respond to – cues to pick up, lines to interrupt – it became almost impossible to learn on my own. The trouble was I had no one to practise my lines against and for a while I even considered taking June, the other girl in the office, into my confidence so that she could say Paul's part, but I realized that would entail telling her the whole story and I could not face that. Finally I bought some blank cassettes and recorded the whole thing at home, saying Matthew's lines myself in as deep a voice as I could manage, then, in my normal voice, my own lines.

Once that was done I spent hours listening to the whole thing over and over again till I was sure that I knew it back to front, then rehearsed it with movements in time to the tape – holding a glass, pretending to eat, resting my head on the sofa-arm as if I was leaning up against him in the taxi on the way home.

But it was hopeless. When I tried to dispense with the tape I found I could not test myself properly; I made another copy, this time reading only his lines and leaving a space where I should speak. It took nearly the three or four weeks until May 6th before I was even moderately satisfied.

In addition to that I spent days looking for a suitable dress. The sort of thing that he had mentioned in his letter was now long out-of-date and I got some pretty odd looks from shop-assistants that I asked. To save my embarrassment I concocted the story that it was for a play in which I had a part – which in a sense I suppose it was – but I still felt a fool whenever I had to ask. In the end I found one, a hair-piece as well, and got dressed up in front of the mirror at home. At first it was quite a shock – I collapsed into girlish giggles, saw in a flash again the absurdity of the whole scheme, then realized I was really rather fanciable like that. The long raven-black hair set off the brown of my eyes – I wondered why I had never considered growing my hair.

By May 6th I was all set. It was to be an unforgettable night.

Ten

Quite in what sense it was to be unforgettable I was not to know until too late. I realize my mistake now of course, but at the time I was just too inexperienced; I was simply a novice at the job.

My downfall was nothing more subtle than sheer over-confidence. God only knows what had possessed me, but when I stepped out of the taxi that night and strutted across the pavement to the restaurant entrance, I pictured myself as some *grande dame* of the stage, expecting everyone to swoon at my feet. I suppose it must have been my 'reviews' – what Fox had written in his letters had gone to my head: he had been 'very impressed' with my first performance, and the second time I'd been 'magnificent', 'exactly' what he had wanted. My lapses, admittedly few, had been curiously erased from the record; I felt sure I was a natural, instinctive actress and there was nothing he could throw at me that I would not be able to handle.

So, as I approached the door of the restaurant, I did not feel nervous – I felt perhaps a faint tingle of excitement, but no quaking at the knees, no fluttering of the heart: none of the symptoms I'd experienced on the previous occasions. It should have been a warning to me. Later I would have taken heed, for I understand now that you cannot achieve your best performance without that kick of adrenalin, that extra shot in the artery. Instead, I was vaguely amused at the whole prospect, I had chatted and joked with the taxi-driver on the journey and the couple of harmless cocktails I'd tossed back before coming out had left me feeling a little light-headed. In addition to that I was already fifteen minutes late. I got exactly what I deserved.

The expression that the doorman threw me should have been a further warning. He was a trim Italian in a bloated frilly dress-shirt. He opened the door as I reached it.

'Good evening, Madam,' he said. 'Do you have a booking?'

His voice was smooth and practised.

'I'm meeting a gentleman in the bar,' I answered.

He inclined his head slightly. 'Of course.'

Thinking back I'm sure I must have imagined it, but at that very moment I could have sworn there was the trace of a sneer in the corner of his mouth. His choice of words seemed to suggest: 'Yes, and I can guess why you're meeting.' It unsettled me minutely. I thought: it can't be obvious, I'm Juliet, not Shirley now. I hesitated, then found my voice.

'Is it through here?' I asked. Again there was the suspicion of a sneer, but he turned aside and showed me the way.

It was at that point I made my second mistake. No doubt it was to spite the doorman in part as well, but as I reached the doorway, I glanced inside to the bar and saw Fox sitting on the far side perched on a stool, back to me, and I was overcome by a sudden flash of petulance. He looked so secure, so nonchalant in his posture that I thought: no, if this bloody script is so vitally important, you can wait; you don't own me: you haven't paid for everything. I turned back to the doorman.

'Oh I'm sorry, I'd like to freshen up first.'

Again he inclined his head. 'As you wish.'

He ushered me through to the back of the restaurant, then departed with the hint of a bow, faintly condescending. I was tempted to make a remark, but then thought better of it.

The toilets were stuffy and airless; there was no window, just stinging strip-lighting and the moment I entered I knew it had been a wrong move. I was suddenly disorientated. I had no reason to be there, I should have got straight on with the performance, and I was irritated with myself. For a time I went through the motions of checking the hair-piece, but it was pointless; I had spent an unnecessary length of time dressing and although I prodded and picked there was nothing to do. Next I looked at my watch. It was 11.35. I was no longer sure this would reassert my authority.

It was while crossing the restaurant to the bar that I had the first premonition things might go wrong. I don't know why the idea occurred to me; it was just a nagging doubt at the time, a kind of omen, like a bottle smashing in the dressing-room. I knew I had been a fool but by then it was too late; it just meant I was already unsteady when the next blow came.

That really shook me. I walked into the bar, came to a halt, and cast my eyes over to the spot where he'd been. According to the script, he was to swivel round immediately and call out 'Juliet'. He didn't. I looked in horror at the stool. It was empty. There was a lump in my throat suddenly and I felt the moment recede. He had gone.

In one desperate glance I took in the room. There were one or two couples seated at tables in the corner, lounging back in easy chairs and chatting as they read through the menu, and the barman was pouring some brandies to pass through the hatch to the restaurant. But Fox was nowhere to be seen.

Instinctively I glanced at my watch, already knowing the time, the truth of what had happened quite apparent. He'd given up waiting, that was all. The explanation was not in any way complex; he'd given me fifteen minutes to show and when I didn't he'd left. All of a sudden I was aware that I must have looked absurd. My grand entrance had rebounded on me; I was standing there just inside the entrance, legs locked and mouth gaping open. The incident could only have lasted a couple of seconds at most, but it seemed a lifetime; I dithered, then realized I had no choice but to leave.

Then, as I was on the point of turning, he spoke. His voice

seemed to boom out above the hushed discussions at the tables.
'Juliet! Over here!'

I suppose the call was not really that loud at all, it had just
surprised me; it came from behind, a corner I had missed when
I strode into the room. I swung round.

'Juliet, your were marvellous!' he said.

The dialogue had started, but already I was lost. He was
approaching me with arms held out in greeting. I tried to work
out how I had missed him; he must have moved over there
simply because I was late – but whatever it was my concentration had gone. He was beaming at me, eyes shining.

'Honestly, you were terrific. Absolutely fantastic! Congratulations!'

I tried to halt him. I could see the seated couples staring up at
us.

'Well go on – say something,' he urged me.

There was a deathly silence. I knew it was my line; that the
last had been scripted to refer to a smile of false modesty I was
meant to be wearing but had failed to express. A vein was
throbbing in my temple and I began to feel hot.

'I . . . er . . . ' Each second became elongated. 'I . . . '

He gave me a couple of seconds more, then leant forward and
prompted. There was an urgency in his voice.

'"It's very sweet of you . . . "' he said.

I nodded dumbly and uttered the line. 'It's very sweet of you,
Paul, but I don't believe it.'

He shifted agitatedly from one foot to the other, then tried to
rekindle the mood. 'No, honestly Juliet! You absolutely stole
the show. You should have heard the comments as we were
coming out.'

It was overdone. In trying to make up for me his enthusiasm
was too forced and I saw the lines for what they were – out of
context – ludicrous, amateurish, from some village hall. Yet
still he expected me to go on.

Again I forgot.

He frowned. '"Well it's very kind of you . . . "'

I repeated it with the first stirrings of anger audible in my

89

voice: 'Well, it's very kind of you to say so,' then stood and waited for his next. My arms were hanging down by my sides, limp, doll-like.

Suddenly he swivelled round. I had completely forgotten what was scripted to follow. He was leaning down to his seat, then straightening up and thrusting a bunch of roses in front of my face. I remembered – the flowers had been scripted – but it was the last straw. I was aware of the people around us. They were peering up, frowning, mystified expressions on their faces.

I expelled a breath. 'Oh my God.'

'Er . . . these are for you,' he said.

I stared at the flowers, then up at him. He was holding them out to me, waiting for me to take them, a pathetic imploring look playing across his face, as if he knew that it had gone too far, yet still refused to admit it. But I'd had enough. I gave a kind of weary snort and at last broke from the script.

'Is it really worth continuing?' I said slowly.

He looked bewildered for a moment but did not speak. I had to go on.

'I mean, there doesn't seem much point, does there?'

His confusion continued a secor two longer – as if he were trying to work out whether this was indeed the script and he'd merely made a mistake – but then his face fell. The hand holding the flowers dropped to his side.

'Why don't you just tell me what it is that you want,' I said. 'It can't be that extraordinary.' The hush in the room seemed to focus in our direction and the barman, who was drying glasses, froze. 'Surely we don't have to continue with this ridiculous play-acting.'

To give him his due, when he saw what was happening he managed to get out with as much dignity as it was possible to salvage from the occasion. I should have guessed what he would do. I suppose it was the only thing he could do in the circumstances, but it was the reaction I'd least expected. He marched straight out of the bar – he did not wait to argue or even bother to curse, he just turned on his heel and made directly for the door. And, as ever, I did the worst thing I could have done: I simply stood there and watched him go. As he swept through the doorway I was briefly aware of a sense of déjà vu – his hair bobbing up and down – then he was gone. One moment he had been with me, the next I was alone.

God only knows how long I stood there looking stupidly after him. Suddenly I remembered all the people who were watching. They were staring up at me in silence, fascinated, and I felt myself go crimson. There was a stifled snigger from one, then another spoke loudly – too loudly, as if to pretend that he hadn't seen the spectacle. I knew I had to do something. I opened my mouth to speak, to apologize or give some hopeless explanation, but managed to stop myself in time. I turned to the bar, then turned back. Finally I decided to go after him.

It was another mistake: I should have just gone home. Instead, I snatched up the roses from the table and rushed towards the door. For a couple of seconds I pushed frantically at it, then understood I should pull. There was a burst of laughter from inside the bar, then I was in the street.

I was only just in time. I could see him in the distance, walking fast and with determination. He had reached the corner with Shaftesbury Avenue and was just about to turn. I lost sight of him. The pavements were still busy, even that late tourists were shuffling around Soho, gawping in the sex-shop windows or dawdling outside the strip-clubs. I blundered up the street colliding into people as I went. Next I started to run. I didn't know what I would say when I caught him; I simply wanted to stop him. I felt so humiliated and so frustrated. Whatever I did he was always one move ahead. If only I could get him to explain.

But it was no use. I arrived at the corner panting, and looked down towards Piccadilly. He had disappeared. In the distance I saw a taxi pulling away from the kerb and for a second I considered stopping a cab myself. Then I gave up. I couldn't catch my breath, and in the ridiculous hair-piece and make-up I felt hot and a little faint. I took another couple of steps forward and stopped. Suddenly I noticed the flowers I was holding. For a moment I couldn't imagine why I had them with me, then I understood. In your most vulnerable moments, habits instilled from childhood can surprise you. With me this was one: an instinctive hatred of wastefulness, the idea that throwing away anything was wrong. My father would never shut up on the subject: all that stuff about pennies and pounds. With one savage wheeling of my arm I hurled the bunch of roses into the gutter and walked away myself.

It's hard to explain, but when I awoke the following morning my anger had almost entirely dissipated. Sleep in its mysterious way had drained me of all the venom and left me feeling empty and, in a sense, ashamed.

I lay there for a long time staring up at the ceiling and watching the breeze stir the curtains, unaware of what the time was and not really caring; not thinking of anything in particular, not even turning over in my mind the events of the previous night, the acting fiasco.

It was a slow-moving morning, the light diffused and pale through the window, the colours mute, anaesthetic. I listened as cars accelerated past outside and women wheeled their prams along, shouting at their other children to stop dawdling. Someone who was whistling spoke when greeted and I recognized the window-cleaner. The world was bearable at this distance, petty and somehow impotent. Nothing seemed to happen, the minutes ticked by into hours, nothing changed or appeared important. At some point I heard the radio drone out as one of the windows below was opened, the fuzzy warmth of the newsreader's voice quite imperturbable.

At last, at about twelve o'clock, I got up and ran a bath. I took a great stack of magazines into the steamy closet with me and wallowed there, letting the heat soak through to my bones until the water became too tepid to stay any longer. Then I dressed, made an omelette and began tidying up the flat. It was to be a cleansing in every sense. A couple of regular clients telephoned but I told them I was feeling unwell and asked them to call back again in about a week's time.

When there was no more to clean up I finally went over to the script. It had been lying on the table since the previous night's last-minute check. I picked it up and took it over to the waste-paper basket, holding it there for a few seconds before dropping it in. I glanced at the first lines again: 'Juliet! You were marvellous! Honestly, you were terrific!' For a moment I tried out a laugh to see how it would sound on my lips, to see if it felt right, but I couldn't convince myself that there was anything funny. I let the script slip from my fingers and watched it fall into the basket, landing twisted and curled. It was a mistake – I should have taken it straight down to the dustbin where the first script had gone.

Next I went over to the cassette-recorder and ejected the tape. It popped out with a loud clack. I tossed it at the basket, but it missed and skated across the floorboards, clattering. I didn't bother to retrieve it.

The final mistake was in deciding to return the cheque. I felt that I didn't want to owe him anything – I wanted to cut all the ties I had with Sylvia Rivers and Juliet Kent. I took the cheque from the drawer, found some writing paper and sat down at the table over by the window. I gazed out for a moment, then started writing, the words going down the moment I though of them:

Dear Mr Fox,

I enclose the cheque for £300 which you sent me to cover my services. Since I did not provide any 'service' I think you should have it back. I certainly don't need any of your money.

I don't know what you're playing at and I don't think I particularly want to either. I'm very sorry if you were not impressed by my performance at Antonio's but I am usually more memorable in another role. If you would like to see a performance of this I'm sure it can be arranged; it is certainly not as perverted as whatever you have in mind.

I'm terribly sorry to inform you that I won't be able to

undertake any more assignments for you but I'm a very busy woman and cannot afford to waste any more time.

Yours faithfully,

SYLVIA RIVERS (MS)

P.S. If you would like a memento of our stage career together this is also perfectly possible: you will find Juliet's hairpiece at Piccadilly Circus Underground in amongst the rest of the shit at the bottom of the ladies' toilet.

I read the letter through once, then crumpled it into a tight ball and threw it at the basket. It also missed.

Later that afternoon I took another sheet of paper.

Dear Mr Fox,

I'm sorry for what happened at Antonio's last night, but I'm not a very good actress. I suppose I was just not expecting it to be quite like it was and when you surprised me there in the bar my mind went a total blank. I apologize if I embarrassed you in front of all those people and would like you to keep the cheque because I don't think I've earned it.

I didn't get any further. It was just no good pretending; I wanted to do it. I ripped the page from the pad and started on another sheet, writing very quickly, before reason had a chance to convince me that I was being foolish.

Dear Mr Fox,

I am very sorry for what happened last night. If you are prepared to take the risk I would like to try again. If you aren't, here is the cheque. I will quite understand.

SYLVIA RIVERS

On a last impulse I wrote in brackets my telephone number and full address.

I folded the letter immediately, put it with the cheque into an

94

envelope addressed to Box 14 and ran down to the post-box.
When it was done and I was back in the flat, I took the script out
of the basket and put it in a drawer for safe-keeping.

I can't honestly say I expected him to answer my letter. It was
written more as a farewell: just to let him know that I was sorry.

Nevertheless, each afternoon when I returned home from
work I went straight to the mail-box and despairingly pushed
my hand inside. It was my last hope. It was as if I were checking
a nest, each day praying there had been an egg laid inside and
each day having to withdraw my hand empty, disappointed. I
went through agonies.

Yet, incredibly, on the tenth day there was something there.
I extracted a slim envelope, looked at the handwriting and then
raced upstairs.

Once more the letter was written in the same polite formal
style, almost business-like.

Dear Ms Rivers,
    Thank you for your letter of May 7th, it was good of
you to take the trouble of returning the cheque.
    I feel that I am partly to blame for the events at
Antonio's – clearly I surprised you by being out of
position at the start of the dialogue, but since you were
late I had moved over to the table so that I could see you
arrive. I now realized that you must have already been in
the restaurant – this is sort of misunderstanding which can
arise when instructions are not followed precisely.
    I am grateful to you for the offer of your services and
after considering the matter carefully I have come to the
conclusion that the assignment is worth attempting once
more. I hope we can put this regrettable incident behind
us.
    I am therefore returning the cheque to you herewith,
and I trust that the further sum will cover any expenses
that you incurred on the 6th.
    Although I have various reasons for wishing to use

95

Antonio's again, I don't think this would be advisable, so I have booked a table at La Luna on Curzon Street for May 23rd. I hope this is not too short notice.

The same arrangements as before are in order.

Yours sincerely,

PAUL FOX

I looked at the cheque he had enclosed. It was now £350. Suddenly, it seemed, life had a meaning again.

Eleven

In parts at least, the evening of May 23rd was a stunning success. Of course my 'talent' was not fully developed by that stage – I did not gain complete mastery of the role until the very last night – but even then I was good, though I say it myself. I was beginning to find my way in the character, beginning to succumb to it – in a sense, I suppose, live it.

This time, as the taxi sped through the streets to La Luna, I became frighteningly nervous. I had worked at the part a lot more over the intervening time and genuinely attempted to put myself in Juliet's place, to imagine how she felt.

Now, as 11.15 approached and the moment that I must walk into the restaurant came closer, I began repeating over and over to myself that word from his first litter: 'glitter', keying myself up for my entrance. You are elated, Juliet, I said; you have barely been off-stage an hour and the adrenalin is still pumping round your system. You cannot keep still. You fidget with your ring, keep touching your hair. The air you breathe seems rarefied, you laugh exultantly, you feel as though you're on a different plane from those around you. This time I was determined to succeed.

It was a warm evening and the atmosphere of the streets helped. There were a lot of couples out strolling, lightly dressed in shirt-sleeves with pullovers draped over their shoulders, and they sauntered along arm-in-arm continental style; there was a feeling of summer and long evenings. As I stepped from the taxi the driver said a cheery goodbye and it buoyed me up – at last things seemed destined to go right.

La Luna was a very similar place to Antonio's, but on this occasion there was no doorman to usher me in. I swept through the door, not confident this time but acting confidence – a subtle difference which I was beginning to appreciate. The restaurant was through to the left, once again darkened, lit only by candlelight. I could see the warm glow on the faces of those eating and noticed as I passed a young woman of my own age laughing, genuinely amused, but silent through the glass. I thought suddenly, I must be like that: carefree and natural, almost abandoned in my laughter.

To the right was the bar. Evidently this was where you browsed through the menu, warmed up over a drink, and I guessed that this was why Fox had picked the place.

A waiter hurried from the restaurant and took my coat, but this time I did not bother to check my hair: it was almost exactly 11.15 and I knew he would already be seated at the bar. In sending my letter I had subconsciously agreed to the rules of his game. Punctuality was clearly one of them. I walked straight in.

This time I had no trouble finding him; he was seated on a high stool at the bar, back to me, smoking.

From that very first moment when he swung round I was sure that I had got it right. There were no other couples waiting and the comparative privacy of it all calmed my nerves.

He approached with those same opening lines, an unconcealed flush of pleasure filling his eyes.

'Juliet, you were marvellous!' he exclaimed. 'Honestly, you were terrific! Absolutely fantastic! Congratulations!'

He paused to give me time to express Juliet's feigned embarrassment, then continued.

'Well, go on – say something.'

I bit my lip. 'It's very sweet of you Paul, but I don't believe it.'

He gave a dismissive wave of the hand. 'No, honestly Juliet. You absolutely stole the show. You should have heard the comments as we were coming out.'

'Well it's very kind of you to say so . . . '

He turned around to get the roses. I felt myself bubbling over with nervous giggles and bit my lip again. This time I did not collapse. As he handed me the flowers his face broke into a funny boyish smile.

'Here, these are for you.'

'For me! Oh Paul, you shouldn't have.' I gazed at him wide-eyed. 'I don't know what to say.'

'Well, don't say anything then.'

I breathed in the fragrance, then put them down and leant forward to kiss him. He offered me a check almost fatherly and I just touched my lips against it.

'Roses! You great softie!'

'I thought –'

'I was only teasing. They're lovely! It's the sweetest thing anyone has done for me for ages.'

'I was going to throw them on to the stage at the curtain-call.'

'I'm glad you didn't. I'd have probably thought they were tomatoes and ducked or something.'

'No you wouldn't – you know how good you were.' He winked, then immediately moved on. 'Anyway, how about a celebratory drink? What will you have?'

I perched myself on the stool beside him and put on a Shirley Temple voice. 'Can I have a big, big glass of wine please, mister?'

He laughed. 'Red or white?'

'White and very dry,' I said in my normal voice. 'I'm just about to die of thirst.'

He turned away to call the barman over and I had a few seconds to think. It was going perfectly, better than I could possibly have dreamed. It was all a matter of the start – if you

99

hit the right tone at the outset then the words seemed to flow, did not seem strained. Don't lose it, I said to myself, just keep going and you'll be all right.

There was a delay while the barman opened a new bottle of wine and there being nothing scripted we had no choice but to remain silent. Out of the corner of my eye I watched him nervously playing with his cigarette, continually rolling the tip against the ashtray to remove the fresh ash as it formed. He was dressed more ostentatiously than on the previous occasions: in light summery clothes – a cream jacket and fawn trousers, a slightly loud green shirt and yellow tie – the shirt and tie a touch more extravagant that his usual dress, a hint of the university world showing through, I supposed. It did not really suit him.

At last the drink came and he handed it to me.

'Are you hungry?' he asked.

I had to concentrate. 'Hungry! I'm absolutely starving!' It was not true: my nerves had killed all the appetite I'd had, but all the same I did my best to sound eager. 'It's crazy, I can't eat a thing before a performance, but afterwards . . . well you just wait and see. You don't know what you've let yourself in for.'

'I think my bank balance will stand it.'

'Well, I'll pay for the wine.'

'Don't be stupid, you won't.'

'Why not?'

'Because . . . I invited you out.'

'You didn't.'

'Er . . . yes, well . . . '

'We'll go halves or not at all . . . '

'We'll see. Anyway. I'm older than you.' He grinned. 'Look, Juliet, I've taken the liberty of ordering for both of us. I hope you don't mind, but the cook here does a wonderful steak. Is that all right?'

'That sounds lovely.'

'Are you sure? I only did it because it was so late. We can change it for something else if you want.' He paused, then continued somehow carefully: 'It's your night tonight, you know.'

He slid me a look. I hadn't paid much attention to the line before but his eyes caught mine slyly as he took a sip of his drink. Clearly he was enjoying the performance.

'No, that's fine,' I said.

He nodded. There was a tiny pause then he went on: 'Well, I didn't realize you could act that well. I thought you'd be good, but not brilliant.'

'I'm not brilliant.'

'That final scene was magical.'

'You're trying to flatter me.'

'I'm not. Believe me – you've got a big future.'

I caught his eye again. He looked away.

'You should have come last night,' I said.

'Why?'

'It was a disaster – you'd never say that if you'd seen me in last night's fiasco.'

'Why, what happened?'

I took another sip of wine and went on to tell him. It was a tale about how my dress – that is Juliet's dress – had become caught on a piece of the set and all the trouble she'd had in trying to disentangle it. It was not particularly important in itself and there were none of the previous ambiguities, it was just something to occupy the time while we finished our drinks. Nevertheless it was my first real soliloquy – and I threw myself into it, jumping down from the stool to demonstrate (I had carefully rehearsed) and by the time I had finished he was roaring with laughter. I think it must have been even better than he could have imagined it for he seemed rapt in my performance as I pranced around pretending to tug at the dress. I was almost disappointed there was no audience other than him to see it – I had even astounded myself.

When I had drained the last mouthful from the glass he suggested that we go in to eat. As we walked through I realized that he must have arranged with the restaurant for them to hold the table for us, for the usual practice was that you were called when your first course was ready. Here there was no waiting, we walked in and were met by a waiter hovering near our table.

I nearly lost it there. According to the script Fox was to seat me, but now the waiter was brushing down the chair and holding it back for me to sit. I looked over to Fox desperately, suddenly afraid I would muff it all once more, but he must have seen my growing panic for he simply nodded that I should let the waiter seat me and then skipped a couple of lines that had been scripted. It was so easy – though I did not know it then – at that stage I was still terrified of departing from the script in even its most minute detail, while he carried on as if nothing had been missed.

'Right, are we going to move on to some red now, or do you want to stick to the same?'

'No, red, that'll be fine.'

He turned to the waiter and ordered a bottle of Saint Émilion. There were a few lines about the restaurant and then we sat in silence watching each other closely while the waiter opened the bottle he had fetched.

It became almost a staring competition, a game to see who would crack the first for he had scripted it so that he should be the first to look away. It crossed my mind that he had done this intentionally, to boost my confidence, so as to prepare me for the next part of the script. It fitted in with the picture I had made of Juliet's character as well: she might grin and snigger but she would not be the first to break. And it had a strange effect: as I stared at him and met the smile in his eyes with the laughter I feigned in mine, there was a transference of this to my mood. I felt a little devilish, more Juliet than Shirley.

At last he looked away and I had the opportunity of glancing round the room as well. There was only one other couple seated near us, all the others were on the far side of the room, near the windows, and they were talking quietly, not in the least interested in us. Once again our privacy helped, I did not feel so exposed.

The waiter filled my glass and went away.

'*Santé!*' said Fox.

'Cheers.'

I raised my glass, clinked it with his and took a sip. The wine tasted velvety and heavy in my mouth as I swallowed. I replaced the glass.

'Paul?' I said quietly.

'Yes?'

I shuffled in my seat. 'I'm not quite sure how to ask this.'

He gave a short laugh. 'Really? You don't usually have any trouble asking questions.'

'What do you think of me?' I said quickly.

'My God, Juliet! You do have a way with the overwhelming questions.'

'No, go on, tell me.'

He pushed his seat back a little and placed his hands on the tablecloth. 'Well, I think you're . . . very . . . I think you're very nice. I wouldn't be here otherwise, would I?'

'Yes, all right, but what do you think of me? I mean, what do you think I'm up to?'

He raised his eyebrows and whistled through his teeth in the same way as he had done at the Tate when I'd surprised him then.

'Come on,' I insisted.

He seemed to search around for words. Suddenly I saw what he was doing: he'd reversed the positions completely, pre-empted any questions I might have about his motives by pretending I'd instigated the whole thing. The game was played throughout so I was the active one – he took the passive role, made out I was leading him. It confused me, made any objections I might have seem useless. I was out-manoeuvred: as script-writer he held all the cards.

'I haven't really thought about it,' he said finally.

'Of course you have.' I had no choice but to go on. 'You must have done. You think I'm trying to seduce you, don't you?'

'This isn't very fair you know, Juliet.'

'I know it isn't. But answer the question all the same.'

He smirked with a kind of shy embarrassment. 'Well, it had crossed my mind I suppose.'

'There! I knew it. And?'

'And what?'

'What conclusion did you come to?' I said.

He threw up his hands. 'You can't ask me that!'

'I just did.' I leant forward evilly. 'You think I've got a thing about older men, don't you?'

'No!'

'You think I'm simply searching for a father-figure to guide me through these wicked times.'

'I don't! That's ridiculous.' He glanced from side to side frantically. 'Must we carry on with this?'

'I just want to clear the air, Paul; make it clear exactly where we both stand.' Like hell, I thought.

'Well you tell me then,' he said suddenly, leaning forward.

'All right then, I will.' I took a breath and winked. 'We're just good friends.'

He spluttered into his wine. It was like a pin exploding a balloon; we both hooted with laughter nervously, all the tension evaporating in a second.

'That's what I thought all along,' he said smiling.

Again I saw what he had done: he had defused the whole subject. Nothing had been answered of course, but by broaching the subject, pretending it had been answered, it did indeed feel as though the air had been cleared. I felt more relaxed, less antagonistic towards him.

'I don't want you to think I'm expecting some kind of pay-off later on, that's all,' I added.

'The idea never occurred to me at all,' he said and smiled again.

'No . . . well, never mind . . . '

It was over. You clever swine, I thought, then had to go on. It was a lighter, unimportant section.

'Anyway, tell me what you thought of the other actors. I'm dying to hear.'

There followed a fairly hefty chunk of the dialogue where we went back to discussing the play, Paul speaking mostly. The first course arrived as well – prawn cocktail, and I launched into mine with much more appetite than I'd expected. As we ate and

104

I was limited to merely prompting him with occasional questions I managed to consider what had happened more broadly.

Clearly something had changed. Almost imperceptibly I was being bluffed into feelings I had not anticipated: in actually uttering to his face the lines he'd scripted, I was being led into the position ofJuilet: the deeper we went and the further the scripts progressed, the more our time relationship of call-girl to client was being whittled away. I felt I was becoming ensnared; I knew I was slipping into some trap, but what kind, and for what purpose?

At the time however there were other things on which to concentrate – the meal and all the incredible complexities that acting while eating entailed.

It was in fact an extraordinary feat of synchronization. Foolishly I had not really given it very much consideration while rehearsing, but there were a number of times when we had to coincide with external events totally beyond our control – the arrival of the food for example, a salad that had been forgotten, the topping up of glasses and the occasion when the candle on our table finally flickered out and had to be replaced.

They were heart-stopping moments. Each time I feared that I would lose the thread, forget where we were in the script, but I survived. It was mainly, of course, because he was doing most of the talking: it was during this time that he told me his life-story. He talked about the play naturally, other plays, questioned me – well, Juliet – about my future and a little about where I was from, that sort of thing, but in the man he talked, about himself, his house and photography, and all I had to do was nod.

But there were other problems as well. I see now how clever he had been to keep the references to the meal itself to an absolute minimum – if the script had been natural in that sense we would soon have been in a dreadful tangle. I have visions of ghastly errors that might have occurred but didn't: referring to the tastiness of the steak before it was served, that sort of thing.

Occasionally he would throw in a spontaneous comment

– unscripted – things like, 'Do you like the meat?', 'More salad?' – tiny deviations from the script with which I could cope, but they were always where there was a short gap, a silence, for otherwise I would have been quickly unsettled.

It was difficult enough trying to make sure I did not deliver my lines with a mouthful of food. On one occasion I did and nearly choked on some meat – then, for one ghastly moment I felt that old panic returning as my mind went a blank.

But I did not forget my lines and I did, in some fashion or other, manage to keep up most of the early elation and glitter. There was a sparkle there, some way in which the surroundings and circumstances rubbed off on our chatter: I felt more and more prepared for the scripted end to the evening, and not with resignation.

There was one section of the script which seemed to echo this. It was after we had finished the main course and were waiting for the sweet.

'What I don't understand', he said, 'is how you can go up there on stage at all.' He was fingering his glass, tracing his finger round the rim. 'It would terrify me. Why do you like it so much?'

'Vanity mainly, I imagine,' I answered. 'Being the centre of attention, in the spotlight – all that kind of thing, you know.'

He gave me a long look. 'I don't believe you're that vain. There must be some other reason as well.'

'You don't know me well enough; I've got the biggest head of anyone you'll have ever met.'

He smiled.

'But you're right, there are other things as well.'

'Such as?'

I began to play with the tablecloth, ironing it flat with my hand, then looking up. I had practised the movement a hundred times, trying to look misty-eyed, Garbo-liked.

'Well, I'm not sure how to explain it exactly,' I went on suddenly. 'It's magical. When you're up there on stage, you're on a high, in a sort of super-sensitive state.'

I glanced at him to see how I was doing. There was a strange trace of amusement about his eyes again and I was almost distracted.

'It's as if you are on drugs,' I said. 'You can feel everything. You notice the minutest details, everything takes on an extra reality – a special kind of reality. You know, you've worked yourself up so much, all the rehearsals, the learning of your lines, the hours and hours you've spent practising movements over and over again, and they've all been leading up to this one moment – and then suddenly you're there and doing it, and you're concentrating so hard that you are conscious of absolutely everything. You know what you're going to say and what you're going to do, so in a sense you don't have to think about it – you can concentrate on experiencing it instead.'

I glanced across at him once more. He was loving every minute of it.

'You can feel the tiniest things; I don't know: the way your shoes feel on your feet, the texture of the dress you're wearing, the way a hair tickles the back of your neck. Does it sound crazy?'

He shook his head quickly, 'Not at all.'

'And then the weirdest part of all is that once it's over, the feeling goes – not immediately – but slowly, coming down; you gradually sink back to a normal state again and you can't remember how those sensations were exactly, you can't recall quite how you felt.'

He nodded.

'It's a bit like making love actually,' I said. I caught his glance, wondering if this had also been scripted to tease. And yet I felt an odd tingling thrill run through me from the acting – there was a sense in which I knew the comparison to be a good one. 'That's the nearest thing I can compare it to – does it shock you?'

He smiled and shook his head slowly.

'It's the same sort of heightened awareness, and the same sort of unreality afterwards,' I continued. I picked up my glass of wine a little nervously. 'Sorry, you must think I've completely flipped my lid.'

'No, I don't at all.' He sounded serious.

'And another thing,' I said, 'you change yourself. You lose part of your personality and take on the personality of the character you're playing. I start behaving differently, speaking in the way they would; you know, I almost start to believe the things they believe. It's like being a chameleon.'

'I preferred your first analogy.'

'You would.'

'You made it sound very attractive.' He winked again – unscripted this time – and I laughed.

'Yes, well, you asked me why I liked it.'

We lapsed into silence. It was a kind of conspiracy – one in which I was wittingly participating. Yet at the same time there was some sort of bond between us from the fact of our having shared the scene – I felt that it would be impossible to hate him. Again I sense that I'd been manoeuvred.

A little later the sweet was brought and we went on with the dialogue once more – this time discussing his work, students he'd taught, what he liked about France. I relaxed again, having only a few question-prompts to slip in, mostly just listening and to my surprise having the opportunity to enjoy the sweet itself – a delicious crêpe suzette, wonderfully light, melting in my mouth. The wine had gone to my head a little, I felt slightly fuzzy, a warm haze around my eyes. Clearly this was just the sort of mood he'd envisaged, for by the time the coffee came I was starting to feel pleasantly sleepy – just as the script required.

It was then that I made my only mistake – at least at the restaurant, that is – for in succumbing to that well-fed, satisfied feeling I decided I could afford a cigarette. I reached across to my bag and took out a packet. Almost immediately I was made to see the error. He leant forward like a hawk and spoke sharply:

'I didn't think you smoked, Juliet.'

I stammered for a moment then had the presence of mind to see what he meant and recover. I sighed regretfully. 'Yes, you're right. I'm supposed to be giving up, aren't I?'

'That's what you told me at the pub,' he answered quickly.

'Oh well, never mind – it would have been nice.' I replaced the packet very reluctantly – I was dying for one – yet at the same time felt rather proud that I had kept my head and shown some quick thinking. It was my first experience of ad-libbing I suppose – and it was not to be the last.

There was more talk about Sussex and then the coffee was at last finished. The waiter approached with the pot to top us again but Fox waved him away. In normal circumstances I would have readily had more, but now I was tired and keen to get the last part over. He looked exhausted too.

He drew his hand through his hair and leant back against his seat.

'Does it feel odd to come out with an old man like me?'

'You're not an old man,' I protested quickly.

'Oh come on, I'm old enough to be your father. It must seem strange.'

Again a suspicion nagged at my mind – was this a set-up also, had he designed this piece of dialogue so that the difference in our ages might not seem so unusual once he had mentioned it? I could not tell.

'Well a bit perhaps,' I said. 'But you're not exactly ancient.'

'I'm fifty.'

'That's not ancient.' I paused. 'And besides, you certainly don't seem like my father.'

'Don't I?' He cast me a sideways glance.

'No, you don't,' I said with conviction. It was the first time really: that comparison with my father. I had to go on. 'He wouldn't be seen dead in a place like this for a start, the old bore.'

'Don't you get on with him?' Fox asked.

Suddenly the script seemed personal. In the rehearsals it had not been noticeable, but now? I wondered: what does he know about me, has he been checking?

'No, I get on with him just fine,' I said.

'Oh.'

The matter was dropped. There was a silence.

'It's been a lovely meal,' I said.

'It's been lovely inviting you.'

'But I invited –'

'Don't let's start that again.'

I waited.

'Perhaps we should do it again some time?' I said quietly.

'Yes, I . . . I would like that very much.'

'Well, we'll arrange it for next time you're up in town.'

'Yes.'

A silence. I nodded dreamily to his answer as directed. Most of the other tables were empty now and the waiters were going around collecting up all the unused cutlery and glasses, hinting that they would like to close. I felt that sense of relief again, that we had almost finished, only that last section to go.

He sat up suddenly. 'Anyway, look it's time I took you home. You must be exhausted.'

'Yes.'

'All that sexual energy you've expended tonight.'

I threw him a glance. 'Don't make fun of what I said.'

'I wasn't trying to,' he said, but winked. 'You are tired though, aren't you?'

'Well maybe, just a little.' I attempted a cosy sort of yawn. 'I'm sorry.'

He smiled. 'Here, I'll go and pay the bill.'

I began to protest again but he waved his hand dismissively and went over to speak to one of the waiters at the desk. I slumped back in my seat wearily: I was really tired. The intensity of concentration that had been required through-out the meal now left me shattered – I realized all of a sudden that I had been 'on stage' for almost an hour without a break.

I looked across the restaurant, Fox was stooped over the inner bar writing the cheque, his hair falling over his eyes as he wrote, so that he had to keep brushing it back. I thought about the script and what was to come: there were not many lines left now, but the kiss to finish it. Once again I wondered if it were reasonable: this 21-year-old girl falling for a man in his fifties.

Usually there was some ulterior motive, a catalyst at least: money, the prestige of some higher social class, but here there was none. He had a charm no doubt, he always seemed to be in control to me, but then that was to *me*, not Juliet – I sensed his power might simply be an illusion created by the fact that I had to follow a script. It was so difficult making sure I did not confuse my feelings with Juliet's. But what did she expect? By all accounts she was attractive; she had a boyfriend (though nothing serious she had said), she could have the pick of anyone she wanted. And yet tonight? Tonight, I sensed it was possible. After the heady excitement of the performance anything was possible: she was in love with the whole world. She wanted to be close to people, share the thrill.

Confusedly, for I was not quite sure how I felt myself, I could imagine her in the taxi letting her head fall on his shoulder or takingis hand; drowsy after the rich food and heavy wine, the memory of the spotlights only dimming then.

As soon as he returned I went to get my coat and we left. He must have ordered the taxi for a set time knowing more or less when we would finish the meal, for when we walked out into the street it was already waiting there, engine stopped, the driver smoking. Nothing was said as we got in – immediately we were seated and the door was closed the driver started up the engine and we swiftly pulled away.

Fox and I settled in the back a little primly, close but never touching, and it seemed an absurd situation to me, knowing what was to come. I felt like giggling all of a sudden: the innocent pose, the pretence that the evening would finish in this fashion, and when I sensed a smile beginning to break across my face I had to look away quickly out of the window in order to compose myself.

The streets were still quite busy with traffic although it was nearly 1 a.m. There was a clear moon and with the canopy of streetlamps the road was illuminated brightly but with an unnatural, somehow disturbing wash of colour. I gazed out at it absently, not thinking of anything in particular, then had to make an effort to regain my concentration when I felt a small nudge in my side – a reminder that I was to resume the conversation.

I did not have to act the sleepy voice, it came without any trouble at all.

'Did you ever live in London?' I said.

He half-turned towards me. 'For a short while – before Mary and I were married. Why do you ask?'

'You seem to know it very well.'

'I don't really.'

'But you know your way around all right, all the restaurants – —that sort of thing. For example, you even knew the cook there.'

'Well . . . I eat out a lot whenever I come up to the city.'

'Mum, I suppose,' I answered. I was not quite sure whether to sound suspicious – it came out that way in any case. I snuggled over to him a little. 'When's next time?'

'I'm not sure. I'll have to ring you.'

'Will that be soon?'

He looked across and held my gaze. 'What do you think?'

I smiled gently and let my hand fall on his arm.

There was another silence, then the taxi lurched round a corner and the lights of the city flashed past the window. For a second I wondered where we were going – I had not taken in the implication of the fact that he had not given the driver an address, but I peered out to see if I could recognize the streets. We were heading north, now passing Euston, the direction of my flat.

The material of his summer jacket felt smooth and cool beneath my hand – slightly damp now as my nervousness increased in anticipation of the kiss. How odd, I thought – after all the men who've used my body, that I should feel apprehensive about a kiss.

'When you were married,' I started quietly, 'did you ever have any affividing glass between us and the driver was closed – it made things easier.

'That's another unfair question,' he said.

'Perhaps – but go on, answer.'
'. . . No, I didn't as a matter of fact.'
'Did you love your wife a lot?'
'Yes.'
'And do you miss her?'
'Of course.' His voice was rather distant, almost embarrassed.

It was my cue. I reached a hand up slowly to his face and turned it towards me. His skin felt taut and dry.

'I want to kiss you,' I said softly.

He looked me directly in the eyes, his pupils flashing anxiously with the stroboscopic effect of the passing lights. He did not answer.

Now was the moment. I gently pulled him closer and stretched up to meet his lips.

It was the strangest kiss. In a sense, I both knew and yet did not know what was happening. His mouth was dry and nervous, quivering slightly as I brushed his lips – I felt it all minutely; and yet at the same time, since it was scripted I did not feel I was really there; it was not me but just my body.

But he was urgent. His arms curled round me, then clasped me tightly – I felt he was afraid the moment might escape him; a kind of shudder passed through him. It was as if he were trying to make these seconds last for ever. Then, instinctively, but more out of habit than any real sense of passion, I tried to force my tongue into his mouth. Immediately his teeth clampled tightly together to stop me and I felt rebuffed, surprised; oddly frustrated.

A moment later he broke away, then sat there, still holding me, but staring out in front. I could hear his breathing: an ageing man's, slightly laboured. I knew it had been a mstake: he had not wanted it like that.

I turned him round again, a half-resistance on his part, and pressed my face to his, kissing him again. This time I did not ape passion. It was more innocent, in no sense whorish, almost an adolescent, virginal kiss. I got it right. He began to caress my neck, running trembling fingers over my head. It must have lasted at least a minute.

Eventually we pulled apart. I nestled my head in the crook of his arm. My lips tingled and I felt a tiny shiver run through my body. The acting had thrilled me; it had produced entirely new sensations from those I'd previously had with clients. He must have sensed the strangeness too for he left a longer silence than the script had indicated. At last he broke it, the set lines intruding. They felt wrong.

'Well I don't quite know what to say.'

I sighed. 'Then don't say anything.'

'I think you're . . . '

'No, please don't,' I cut in. 'Don't say anything. Just hold me – like this.'

He nodded.

The rest of the journey we sat in silence. I watched blankly as we raced closer and closer to my street, no longer sure if I would be glad when we arrived there. The kiss had been so totally harmless, his grip on me was so controlled, so asexual: almost a stronger denial that I was being used as a prostitute than if we had simply sat on the extreme sides of the taxi-seat. I felt quite relaxed, just one or two simple lines left. The acid test was over. I think I could have quite happily sat there all night.

Idly, I began to wonder with perhaps a hint of sadness, if this might be the last script. I thought: maybe this was all he had ever wanted – that fresh, girlish, untainted kiss. I wondered if I was some kind of stepping-stone on a sentimental journey: perhaps he was trying to recapture, recreate a childhood sweetheart, some experience he'd had as a boy and could not forget. A tiny stab of jealousy pricked me – all that I had missed; and he was old enough to be my father – he had said it himself.

At last the taxi pulled into my road. We drew up quickly in front of the flats – without any searching for the address. The driver left the engine running and we sat silent for a moment listening to the diesel noisily ticking over. Then Fox spoke.

'Well here we are.' His voice was resigned, also weary.

'Yes.'

He unwrapped his arm from around me.

'Thank you for coming.'

'Thank you for inviting me.' A pause. 'It really was a gorgeous meal.'

'I'm glad you liked it.'

We waited. Juliet obviously did not know how to finish the evening.

'Well!'

Another pause, then she decided. I leant across and kissed him once more – briefly this time – then looked him in the eye.

'You'll call me?'

'I'll call you.'

'Soon?'

'As soon as possible.'

He smiled, eyes alight once more. A last touch on the lips and then I edged across to the door and got out.

'Good night then.'

'Good night Juliet.'

The end of the script. I held my hand on the door, not quite sure when to close it. He nodded at me.

And then, God knows why, I said it. I couldn't stop myself. Momentarily I suppose I misunderstood the nod; maybe not. Maybe I still believed that it was what he really wanted, or maybe it was something else; not wanting to finish it there. But in any case I said it.

'Would you like to come in?'

It was not in the script, and it was a terrible mistake. His jaw dropped suddenly, the sparkle in his eyes clouded over and he lurched across the seat, slamming the door, wrenching it out of my hand as he did so. He banged on the dividing glass inside and the taxi pulled away immediately. I was left standing there on the pavement staring uselessly at the receding lights.

Twelve

That night I could not sleep. As soon as I got in I went straight to bed determined not to think about him, wanting only to forget the whole business and get a good night's rest. I should have done: I was exhausted, there was no doubt of that – as I have said the performance had drained me of all the nervous energy I'd survived on for weeks – but I hovered on the brink of sleep for almost an hour in that strange no-man's-land where you are neither truly awake nor quite asleep. I must have shifted the pillow a dozen times, reversing it again and again in the hope that the coolness of the undersurface would still my thoughts, turning my head from side to side like a child attempting to find a position where a nightmare cannot find a way in.

At last I had to admit that I would not sleep. I would have to think it over – sleep alone would not assimilate the evening.

I switched the light on, sat up in bed, lit a cigarette, then turned off the lamp again and lay back in the darkness, smoking, carefully tapping the ash off into an ashtray by the glow of the tip alone.

I felt guilty. It seems crazy to think of it now – the idea that I was being cheated in some way did not occur to me; instead I thought I had let him down and should be ashamed.

To my horror I discovered that I had completely forgotten about the money. Now, as I lay there in the darkness, it came suddenly home to me: he had paid £350 for that evening – even more if you included the meal and taxis and drink and all the other extras, and I had gone and ruined the whole thing.

Admittedly, my performance had been good – I had seen from his eyes, from his obvious excitement that I had achieved the effect he'd wanted; there had been a few lapses of course, a number of lines that I had not got exactly right, but over all it had been a performace that I should have felt justly proud of – until that final line that is, when I had destroyed everything.

It was not Juliet – I saw it in a flash – she would not have invited him in, not yet at least. She was revelling in the romance of the thing, in love with love, not really with him – she might sleep with him, but not straightaway – it would have been too much of a seduction, far too rushed for the classic affair of which she was dreaming. I had not really misunderstood his nod – it was an excuse that's all; it had been pure selfishness on my part – I had wanted him to come in, I wanted to know more about him and solve the riddle, I wanted to understand the mystery he had created and debunk it; above all I resented the hold he had on me, the way he could manoeuvre me. By bedding him I had subconsciously believed I would outplay him – after that he could be discounted – he would join the ranks of the other sad creatures who'd climbed the stairs up to my flat. It was control that I wanted, nothing more subtle; so I'd played my usual role: the whore. I remembered what the letter had said: 'Do not step out of your role in any way'. I wondered then, my role as who – as Shirley, Sylvia or Juliet?

It was then I suppose that I first understood that Juliet was a real person. God only knows why it hadn't come to me before, but suddenly I realized I'd already said it. Juliet would not have invited him in, Juliet would not have done that. She was not simply a character in a script, not just fiction. There had been

117

plenty of clues all along: the clothes, the hair-piece, the loaded scripts – the insistence that I should not ask questions. I was playing the part of someone from his past, not some carefully constructed idealized vision. Of course, I suppose I'd already had glimmers of all this, but it had never appeared to me so clearly. I had still vaguely imagined I was playing a fantasy figure, some cranky elaborate version of the schoolgirl/pigtails theme. Now everything began to fall into place. He was trying to recreate the past, relive the magical moments in his life, have his time with Juliet all over again. That was the meaning of 'no questions'. If at any time I reminded him I was not Juliet the effect was ruined. Once I stepped outside the role I destroyed the whole elaborate artifice. He was imagining that I was her, reliving every second he'd spent with her consciously, totally aware of what was happening. I myself had explained it in the script – the passage about acting – he knew what was going to happen, so he could concentrate on experiencing it. And clearly she hadn't invited him in for the night; it had ended where the script had finished. With horror I saw my final words had undermined completely the delicate structure of the evening.

I switched the light on once more, got out of bed and fetched the script. Were there further clues? Was this what really had been said? I climbed back into bed and turned to the end.

JULIET (*hopefully*): You'll call me?
PAUL: I'll call you.
JULIET: Soon?
PAUL (*slowly*): As soon as possible.
Pause. Juliet kisses briefly,
moves across to the door and gets out. She stands holding the
door open.
JULIET (*quickly*): Good night then.
PAUL: Good night Juliet.
She closes the door immediately.

Was there a further script? I felt sure there must be. He would not have gone to all these lengths if it had simply ended there;

yes, there must be. But now, after what had happened that night, would he let me play it? Would he take the risk?

I so much wanted to be given just one last chance. I was sure I could play the role: I would immerse myself in the part if only he would let me. With each performance I had improved; I was beginning to understand the kind of girl Juliet was, develop mannerisms, affect a way of speaking. Next time I would be absolutely magnificent; it would be a blinding, unforgettable performance.

I turned off the light again and lay back. My head was swimming. I felt almost drunk: the lack of sleep, the sudden excitement. I remember praying: Please have faith in me, I won't let you down.

Quite ironic really when I think of it now. At some point in that long black night, as sleep at last approached, I realized another thing. I wanted to know what happened. I was as keen to find out how their story ended as I was to be given the chance to act it.

The next fortnight was dreadful: it was the longest wait of my life. By the end of the first week I had sunk into my worst depression. It was not at all that my desire to have the part declined; quite the opposite in fact, it grew more obsessive every day, I could hardly think of anything else – it took over all my waking thoughts and invaded my sleep so much that I had difficulty in deciding which was real and which was dream.

I had my other clients of course but they began to drift away. Suddenly there seemed no point. I no longer derived any enjoyment from duping them; the frenzy and passion I had always feigned was impossible to pretend, there was no kick in it any more and no reason if I didn't need the money. I began to lose them – just one or two of the regulars at first, but a sure decline; I only carried on out of habit.

Each day I checked the mail-box, and each day it was empty. I understood, yet could not believe it. Finally I determined to make inquiries myself. At least I would be doing something.

My first approach was to write to Box 14 again. It was a

pathetic, almost love-lorn, begging letter. I pleaded for a final chance, promised I would never repeat my error, I stooped as low as you can go. It was to no avail. The letter was returned – unopened – with a note from the magazine: Box 14 was now closed; it seemed their client no longer required the service.

Next, the university. I decided to write, then changed my mind. If I rang perhaps I would stand a better chance of convincing him I was really serious. I was not sure exactly what I would say: beg again, I can only imagine, or pretend to be Juliet asking when he was next coming up to town.

Even then, despite my obsession, it was hard to find the courage. I sat holding the receiver in my hand for at least ten minutes daring myself to dial the number before I did so. I got through to a receptionist and asked for Paul Fox in the French Department.

I shhave expected it really. In all the letters there had been no address or telephone number – what would have been the point of withholding those if he were so easy to trace through the university department? He had covered all his tracks. There was no Paul Fox in the French Department; there was no lecturer of that name in any department, no Paul Fox in the whole of Sussex University. It was a shock all the same. Had I got the whole thing wrong? Perhaps he wasn't reliving his past after all, as I had thought; there was neither a Paul Fox nor a Juliet.

I thought again. Maybe he no longer taught there, that was all; yes, if he was reliving his past then it was possible that he'd only taught at Sussex at the time he'd met Juliet. I telephoned again.

This time the receptionist put me through to one of the older members of staff in the French Department. He was very busy and very abrupt. I was trying to trace an old friend I said. I believed that he'd once taught at Sussex – a Paul Fox; could he help? His answer was short and gruff, a hint of 'Is this really so important?' in his voice. No, there had never been anyone of that name in the French Department – he'd been at the university since it opened and if he didn't know him, then no one would. So sorry he couldn't help.

I tried a couple of other possibilities. I rang directory inquiries and asked for a P. Fox in the Brighton area. There were two; neither turned out to be a Paul. Then London – there was a chance that he lived in London: his bank account was here. There were fifteen of them – and I ploughed through them all myself – Peters, Patricks, Philips and Paulas and Paulines yes, but not one Paul. I was not particularly surprised.

I had one last card to play – the bank account itself. For a couple of days I wrestled with my conscience, then gave in to the worse half of my nature. One of my regulars was a bank manager: I asked him to find out about the account. He refused to do it of course, gave me the usual guff about professional confidentiality and said that besides, the account was not even with his bank – it would be impossible for him to get the information. Why was I so interested anyway, he asked? I had been expecting the question. It is the only time I ever used the advantage of my profession for anything that I would consider wrong. I knew it was wrong but I was so obsessed by Fox by that time that I would have been prepared to do almost anything. I assured him that it was nothing criminal, I was not after the man's money or to use the information illegally, but if he, the bank manager, did not get me what I'd asked for, then I was afraid his wife would have to know the real reason he stayed late in the city.

It would seem that getting the information was not as great a problem as he had claimed: it was sent by letter a couple of days later. I would like to say that I felt ashamed.

According to the note, the account was a new one. It was also rather unusual. There had only been one deposit – of £2,000, right at the beginning of April, then just five major withdrawals: one for £350, one for £150 and three for £100 each, and a host of smaller payments. For a moment I was perplexed. The two larger ones I'd received; the smaller payments could be easily explained as train tickets, the meal-bill etc., but of the three for £100 I'd received only one. That was another shock: to realize I'd had two unsuccessful predecessors.

The most important item of information was the address. It was given as 38 Blenheim Rise, Chelsea.

Any celebration I had that night was quite premature. The following morning I took a taxi to the house. I wore the white dress and hair-piece, was very excited and more than a little pleased with myself. Would he be in? What would he say? Perhaps I should just leave a note? I needn't have bothered to think about it. The house existed all right, otherwise I imagine the bank statements would have been returned to the bank, but the place was empty. Through the frosted glass of the front-door panel I could see a scattering of letters. I had pinned my last hopes on the visit. I returned home by taxi in a flood of tears.

After that I gave up even so much as bothering to look in the mail-box when I returned home from work. And that following week I hit rock bottom. I hardly left the flat at all; I told my clients I was ill and could not see them, ate scrappy meals and drank alone in the desolation of my rooms. With that one tiny sentence, that string of six words only: 'Would you like to come in?', so apparently harmless, a phrase yearned after by others, I had lost him.

And indeed I might well have missed my chance for ever had the envelope dropped perfectly into the mail-box. I had given up looking, resigned myself to failure finally; it was only because it was in front of my eyes when I walked into the entrance one afternoon, sticking halfway out having failed to drop cleanly into the box. I pulled it out almost apprehensively at first, then snatched at it and bounded up the stairs to the flat. My depression fell away from me in a second. I could not prevent a small hysterical laugh.

Three things again: a cheque, a script, another letter.

I turned straight to the last.

Dear Ms Rivers,

Thank you for coming to the restaurant on May 23rd. As I am sure you will realize from the long delay between that last meeting and my sending this, I have been carefully considering whether or not to abandon the whole project. I do not think it is necessary for me to explain in detail my reasons – I trust you will realize what I am referring to.

Nevertheless, I have decided to continue. On a number of occasions that night you achieved exactly the effect I had been hoping for – a remarkable feat I must admit since it was an extremely demanding performance. I am therefore asking you if you would be willing to undertake a further assignment – provided there are no more lapses – and I am enclosing another script which I would once again be grateful if you learnt.

The actions takes place as you will see in Hyde Park. I will be waiting at the Bandstand there at 12.30 on June 25th. I hope this date is convenient.

Paul and Juliet have met twice more in the intervening period. On the first of these occasions he has taken her to the theatre and for a meal afterwards; on the second occasion Juliet has cooked for him at her flat. You will notice references to these in the script.

However, despite these meetings their relationship has not changed appreciably – it has continued on more or less the same kind of level.

This time I would be grateful if you would wear jeans and a blue-and-white-striped T-shirt. I am hoping the weather will be fine, but should it not be, bring a denim jacket.

As before I enclose a cheque for your services.

Yours,
Paul Fox

The cheque was for £300 this time, the standard fee, I gathered: the extra £50 for the 23rd had only been for the abortive night when I had broken down.

I picked up the script with almost greater interest. I was eager to find out what happened. It took me almost half an hour, but when I finished it I was smiling wryly. I knew then the answer to the question I had asked myself ever since that first performance; I knew why he had wanted me for the part, and not a real, serious actress.

Thirteen

Unfortunately, for Fox at least, June 25th was not a particularly fine day. When I awoke that morning heavy clouds were lumbering across the sky – the hot spell that had stifled London for the previous ten days had finally broken. Not that it was actually raining – it threatened to all the time – but the wind had whipped up and kept the clouds moving sufficiently fast to hold off a downpour. It was just dull, a rather miserable day, the sort that holidaymakers dread – not at all the weather for T-shirts and lying on the grass in Hyde Park. Of course, Fox said himself in that very script that you cannot recreate the past – external circumstances always intrude to spoil some effect or change some aspect, but it seemed that on this occasion nature was trying to press the point home so that there could be absolutely no misunderstandings.

Nevertheless, I dressed that morning as closely to his instructions as I could manage, wearing the T-shirt I had specifically bought for the performance, but putting on another beneath it; then a scarf knotted at the neck and the denim jacket he had mentioned. I suspected that I was probably going to feel a little cold but was prepared to suffer in the interests of producing an unforgettable performance.

I left the flat at 11 a.m. It did not take more than half an hour to get to Hyde Park from home but I had planned to arrive there well in advance of the time in order to get my bearings, and accustom myself to the mood of the place. There may have been a tinge of the old business of wanting to see him off-stage, seeing the actor out of costume; but it was mainly the former reason: I was eager to put in a thoroughly professional performance.

Of course I had been to Hyde Park earlier in the week to familiarize myself with the settings – the Bandstand, the Serpentine, all the surroundings, so none of it was new to me now, but I felt I wanted to spend some time there just walking around, getting the feel of the Park so that later I would be able to concentrate on the acting. I was determined to succeed, to get every detail exactly right.

There was only one thing that I was still worried about. I don't mean nervous – for I was, thank God, sufficiently nervous anyway to heighten the performance – but worried; the script was not complete. Instead of scripting every word that was to be said, Fox had only written out short scenes which were to be interspersed throughout the meeting. The rest we were to improvise, to act out in the roles of Paul and Juliet.

I could understand why he had done it. Unlike the restaurant where it had already been extraordinarily tricky, it would be absolutely impossible here to fit in exactly with the various practical arrangement – the boats and such like – at least not without some kind of rehearsal together. There was another reason as well, though I did not realize it then – it was to see if I could cope with sustained improvisation, for if I couldn't there wouldn't have been much point in continuing – the final night would have been totally inconceivable as a closely scripted scene. If I had known that I would probably have been even more worried, but as it was I just feared that I would not be able to manage the parts he had not scripted for that morning – I was sure I would dry up, gibber stupidly as I had done in the restaurant the first time, unable to think of things to say.

Despite all this I was still excited. As I walked into the Park from Knightsbridge Station, past the Dell and up towards the Bandstand, everything around me took on a kind of unreality. It's difficult to describe – maybe it was not so much unreal as super-real, in the way that Juliet had described the special magic of acting. All the trees and flowers seemed to force themselves into my consciousness, project themselves forward into prominence like those folding pop-up theatres I remembered from my childhood – cards which, when set up, placed figures in perspective – some in front and some behind, thrown into contrast against a carefully painted background. It was like wearing 3-D glasses: birds swooping down really looked as if they might hit you, a football rolling across the turf appeared to come out of the screen to meet you. Sounds came from all sides in quadrophonic – it was as if I had never seen the world in quite this way before – living, throbbing, each second totally un repeatable.

He was not at the Bandstand when I reached the spot where we were to meet, but I sat down on a bench well away from there and looked around in case by any chance I had missed seeing him. A group of Japanese tourists were photographing one another on the steps of the Bandstand and they were chatting animatedly, pushing one another to the front, then posing stiffly as the picture was taken. One by one they scurried from the group and replaced the photographer until at last with a sudden burst of shrill giggling they moved off, each with his photograph. Some roller-skaters glided up and down the path, pirouetting as they passed, some dancing to music they were playing through tiny headphones.

Only one or two other benches were occupied. At one, a pair of lovers sat talking earnestly. I watched them for a while trying to guess their conversation. The affair was clearly at a crisis: they were both staring at the grass in front of them, turning occasionally to say a few words, then shaking their heads. At one point the boy took the girl's hand with a kind of final desperation, but when there was no response he dropped it. Finally he stood and marched away. The girl watched him go and began to sob softly. I looked elsewhere for a few moments,

embarrassed, then had to look back. She had got up herself and
· was walking slowly off. A little piece of silent theatre.

All of a sudden he was walking past me. He must have seen
me; there was no way that he could have avoided it, and yet he
did not acknowledge me. He had approached from the other
side of the park – the Marble Arch end – not from Hyde Park
Corner as I'd expected for some quite unfounded reason. Once
more I was thrown into complete confusion – he walked round
in front of the Bandstand where the Japanese had been and sat
down on one of the steps. He did not look up at me but I knew I
had to make a getaway. I leapt up and hurried away towards the
lake and cafeteria, a ghastly feeling rising in my throat again.

It was only midday, but I should have guessed he would come
then – it was just stupid of me. In the script, Juliet was meant to
arrive half and hour late for the rendezvous; he had evidently
come on time so as to relive even the experience of waiting for
her. Yet again I'd ruined things – not really out of selfishness this
time, but still another stupid waste – £300 more and another
memory tainted. I felt sure that he would not be there at 12.30,
it would have been the last straw for him, the sorry proof that he
had been wrong to trust me.

I wandered dejectedly along the Serpentine Road up to the
cafeteria and sat down there with a cup of tea, close to tears. If
he wasn't there, I would never forgive myself. The world, that
only a few minutes previously had seemed so alive and pulsat-
ing, was now drab and lifeless, barely a shadow of what it had
been. I smoked two cigarettes in quick succession and stared at
my watch. The second-hand crept round, struggling slowly yet
somehow moving. With each second that passed I sensed that
the chance I'd had and all its possibilities were moving further
away into history. The words that I was primed to say would
never now be uttered, the scripted kisses never acted out. I felt
suddenly cold, angry with myself that I should have been so
crazy as to come to the park in inadequate clothes: absurd in
this situation where everybody around me was warmly-
wrapped. Even if he was there, by the remotest chance, what
would it be like in the boat? I was surely bound to freeze.

At twenty-past I got up from my seat, walked once around the Dell to kill five minutes and then began heading back to the Bandstand. I tried to life myself, to stir the adrenalin: if he was still there, if he had only waited, he would get a performance he would never forget. If . . . always so many ifs.

Of course he had stayed. I could make out his figure almost from the corner of the road though he must have been a good hundred yards away. My heart leapt, though even then I could not be absolutely certain it was him until I was much closer. But it was. He was sitting on a bench now near the edge of the grass, hunched up, head down in the pose of one who's praying after sitting down in church. He looked weary, disappointed. He held his forehead in one hand, massaging his brow and temples with deep, slow, penetrating strokes as though he had a headache. I wondered if he had already started acting.

I sneaked on to the grass behind him and approached as the script had indicated, creeping up with stealthy silent steps so that he would neither see nor hear me. He looked totally vulnerable; I felt he was suddenly in my power. My heart was beating crazily again, my stomach churning. A couple of steps forward. With one swift movement I clasped my hands over his eyes and spoke:

'Guess who?'

He jerked up suddenly. 'Juliet!' His exclamation burst out as if he really hadn't believed it. 'Dear God, don't ever do that again.' He removed my hands from his eyes but continued to hold them. I stepped over the bench and stood in front of him.

'Did you think I wasn't coming?'

'I was just about to give up hope.' He still looked dejected.

Again I sensed that weird role-reversal: as if it had been him and not me sitting so morosely in the cafeteria.

'I'm sorry Paul, I just couldn't get away. Peter wanted us to run through the *whole* of the second act again. Am I very late?'

'Well . . . '

'I am, aren't I? Did you think you'd been stood up?' I said it teasingly but his expression remained sullen.

'It had crossed my mind,' he said.

'Seriously?'

'Why not?' He cast me a long glance but added nothing more.

'I'm sorry. Will you forgive me?' I said timidly.

He did not answer for a moment but seemed to consider the question almost profoundly. Then he looked up. In his eyes there was a trace of craft that I'd not noticed before.

'Perhaps,' he said, then with care: 'but you'll have to show greater contrition than that.' Then he grinned.

It was the cue to kiss him. I hadn't realized until that moment just how cunningly he'd manoeuvred the whole conversation. As I moved across – this as scripted too – and perched myself on his knees I was faintly aware that anyone watching would have seen it all as I had the couple earlier: a little piece of theatre. I was balanced there on his legs like some stage puppet and yet as I leant across and pressed my lips against his I felt quite the opposite. My sensitivity heightened and I weirdly recalled that extra kick I'd experienced from my first-ever proposition. My tongue searched into his mouth instinctively: a trade-practice, I thought afterwards, overruling the memory of the incident in the taxi. On this occasion he did not stop me. He responded by putting a hand up to my cheek and slowly caressing the lobe of my ear. I shivered.

After a few moments I arched away from him a short distance and looked into his eyes. They were soft and watery.

'There – is that enough?' I asked gently.

He smiled, holding my gaze.

'No. I don't think you really mean it.'

The ambiguity caught me by surprise. I grinned and kissed him once again, rather more lengthily than the script had indicated, then pulled myself away, feeling my concentration lapsing.

'That *is* enough,' I said primly. I straightened up, then slipped myself off his knees and on to the bench beside him. My face was flushed and my heart was racing. I was not quite sure who had been doing the teasing any longer, but it didn't seem to matter. I paused a few seconds longer then went on, relieved to feel the safety of the script.

'Right,' I said. 'What shall we do now? How long have you got?'

'About an hour, then I'm due at the conference I'm afraid.' It was said directly – no hint of his former sulkiness.

'Oh God, I'm sorry. I've ruined the whole thing, haven't I?'

'Not at all. It was worth waiting for.'

'I am "by flatterers beseiged".'

He laughed and looked at me. 'Pope?' he said questioningly.

'Yes,' I said slowly. 'Are you sure it's French you teach?'

He smiled but did not take it up.

'Do you want to walk?'

'Yes, all right,' I said brightly. 'Hey no! – what about taking me on a boat on the Serpentine.'

He gave a withering smile. 'So you can lie at the back and trail your fingers romantically through the water while I sit in the middle having a coronary over the oars? Is that it?'

'That's it.' I bounced up from the seat and took his hand. 'Come on Grandad!' I dragged him to his feet.

As we walked to the boathouse the first period of improvisation took place. In fact, he had not scripted anything more until we were settled in the boat, but despite my fears it went quite well – I found it a lot easier than I'd expected. There were indeed plenty of things to talk about: he started by commenting on the roller-skaters, asking me what the headphones were in aid of; then some horse-riders passed, kicking along the the sandy track beside the tarmac and we talked about riding for a while. I made one tiny error only – I told him about the lovers I had watched earlier. Only after I had started did I realize that I was drawing attention to the fact that I had not been 'late' at all, but had arrived before him, but I don't think he noticed – certainly there was no frown, no sudden flinch as on the other occasions. Moreover, when I mentioned, a little daringly, how the scene had resembled something out of the theatre he cast me a sidelong glance and looked faintly amused by what I'd said. I realized immediately that my position had changed after that, there was a sense of conspiracy that linked us – it had been an unconscious admission on my part that I enjoyed the game and was prepared to keep the secret: a subtle progression towards submission.

We had no trouble in getting a boat, there were only three or four others out on the water. It was not the idyllic weather that should have set the scene, but at least it meant that we did not have to wait.

I stepped in and sat down at the back and as he clambered unsteadily to his place I gave the boat a little rock, almost tipping him into the water. It was exactly right, just the touch of improvisation he was hoping for: I knew the girl I was playing by then — the teasing, innocence, the sheer joy at living. He cried out naturally, then saw the funny side; his sudden flashing smile showed that he had appreciated the act. Indeed, I wondered then, if quite by accident, I had happened on something that had indeed occurred: something which he had decided to leave out of the script as being either too tricky to enact or too absurd. He took his place at the oars, wagging his finger paternally.

Fox pushed the boat away from the jetty and then rowed us out for about five minutes and we fell silent for a while. I relaxed, lying back, trying to imagine it as it must have been: a classic backdrop — the sun, the lap of water against the hull, swallows dipping low over the surface of the lake, the occasional cries of youngsters larking in the other boats. I felt a little sad: sorry that it couldn't be like this today, this memory that I had been allowed to share. And yet . . . I remembered what was to come — the distrust and arguing, the sudden temper I had to unleash upon him.

Suddenly he stopped rowing, resting on the oars: the signal for me to resume the script. I was sitting back against the stern, hugging my arms around me from the cold, watching the ducks paddle out of our path as we drifted towards them.

'I wish it didn't always have to be these one-day trips,' I said, affecting a sudden frustration. 'I only see you about once a month.'

'It's more often than that.'

'Well, not much more.' I looked out over the water. 'Anyway, you know what I mean.'

He sighed. 'Yes, I wish it could be more often as well.'

I left a pause.

'Damn it – *why* can't I visit you!'

'We've been through all that before. You know why.'

I looked at him seriously and spoke quietly. 'you were telling me the truth weren't you, Paul? You're not married are you?'

'I've told you. My wife died five years ago.'

'And you've not remarried?'

'And I've not remarried.'

'No mistress secretly stashed away at home?'

'No.'

'Then I can't understand why I can't come down and see you!' I sat up with a jerk, rocking the boat violently with the movement. 'I mean, your children are twenty and eighteen, for Christ's sake! They're adults. They'd understand!'

'They –' He cut himself short. Whatever it was he had in mind to say, he saw it was pointless going on. He shook his head almost despondently.

'What is it? Last time you said they were the reason; you couldn't "face telling the children" or something.'

'Well it's not that.'

He pulled the oars in and the blades dripped with little pats into the water. I waited for him to explain further but it was as if he thought he might get away with nothing more than a denial.

'I'm waiting,' I said.

He sighed heavily. 'You won't believe this.'

'I'll decide what I believe.'

He shrugged and looked away. There was a brief silence, then he said quietly:

'I want to keep you a separate world.'

I looked at him but he avoided my eyes.

'I don't want you to come to my home because if you did the whole thing would be ruined. I enjoy meeting you so much particularly because it's completely separate from everything else. Does that sound ridiculous? Can you understand?'

I observed him lengthily. 'Yes, I think so. I'm your "bit on the side", isn't that right?'

'No!' He paused. 'Be fair, Juliet. It's just that everything that has happened seems to have taken place in some other world. I want to keep it that way.'

I pursed my lips.

'Besides,' he went on, 'I always thought you felt the same.' He threw me a quick glance but gave nothing away.

'Perhaps I did,' I said, then looked out sulkily across the water. I let the words hang for a while, then went on suddenly:

'Anyway, I'm sick of it all. It's becoming boring.'

'I see.'

'I'm being used.' I said it petulantly, still looking away out of the boat as directed, but wanting to see his expression at the same time.

'That's not quite the way I see it.'

'What do you mean!'

'Well you started the whole thing.'

I stared at him incredulously. I was hardly aware that I was acting.

'My God, you've got a nerve! How can you say that? You pick me up on a train, wine and dine me, whisper sweet nothings in my ear till I can't think straight any more and then expect me to say that I started it!'

'You know it wasn't like that at all.'

'All right, how was it then?'

'You pushed the issue – at the Gallery.'

'I was only stating what was bloody obvious.'

'Well maybe some things are better left unsaid.'

'Oh yes?'

'Yes. When you're older perhaps you'll see that.'

I was not sure whether it was Juliet or I who lost her temper then.

'Oh my God, don't start that one! Don't come the wise-old-daddy act with me. I may be thirty years younger than you, but I'm not completely naïve, you know.'

'I know.'

'Well?'

He did not answer straightaway. The boat had drifted in towards the bank and he had to row for a few moments to set it back towards the middle. A group of passers-by were watching us, obviously listening to the dialogue, not quite sure whether to be amused or embarrassed by it all. My heart was beating hard with the anger I had generated for the scene and now it grew more vehement and real as I saw that he was playing with us both again – Sylvia and Juliet. I could hardly wait for him to say his next line so that I could have the chance to burst out once more.

He stopped rowing and began to speak at last, very slowly, weighing each word carefully. 'Listen, Juliet . . . if I were married . . . would it really make that much difference?'

My anger vented. I tried to drag myself to my feet, but fell into a semi-kneeling position.

'You *are* married! I knew it! I knew all along. Christ, Paul – '

He tried to steady the boat. 'I'm not, I've told you. Calm down – you'll throw us both in.'

'Who cares!'

He looked around a little shamefacedly. 'We've got an audience,' he whispered.

'Good.'

He shook his head like a weary father.

'Why didn't you tell me!' I said.

'Listen . . . I'm not married.'

'Then why are you asking how I'd feel about it.'

'Just answer the question.'

'Why should I?'

He held my eyes, staring me out, as at the restaurant. This time he had scripted himself to be the victor.

'Would it make any difference?' he repeated.

'I . . . ' I was meant to check, then change my mind. I spoke more slowly. 'Yes it would, it would mean that . . . oh Christ, I don't know. Maybe not . . . I feel so confused.'

He did not let it drop but looked at me hard, that fierceness again in the usually soft eyes. 'It would be the end wouldn't it?' he said.

I felt the anger draining away. 'Yes, it would.'

'That's all I wanted to know.' He picked up the oars and began rowing again slowly. 'Now let's forget it,' he said.

'But you're not married?' I asked for the last time.

'No.' He caught my eyes for the briefest second, then looked away.

That was the end of the second part of the script. I lay back against the white-painted metal back-rest and relaxed once more. Why, I wondered, should he wish to relive this scene; what pleasure could he possibly derive from living through an argument again? The script had suddenly felt much more natural – the distrust and shouting had taken away a sense of artificiality; the two characters were again more credible. Maybe that was why he had included the scene – he felt that he had to be true to the past: recall the bad times as well as the good so that those magical moments would seem more real.

I watched as he rowed, rhythmically dipping the oars into the water and straining back against them. He was purposefully avoiding my eyes, knowing that I was observing him. Now he did not look as young as he had done in the restaurant; his face was pale, the eyes a little baggy and I noticed the sag of a double chin folding against his collar each time he pulled on the oars. A likeness to my father struck me suddenly – they were the same age; that chin much more similar than I had previously noticed. I felt a tiny dart of bitterness prick me.

I looked away finally and we rowed on in silence, the wind picking up once more so that I had to pull down the cuffs of my jacket over my hands to stave off the cold. I glanced up at the sky feeling a few spots of rain and nervously wondered what would happen if there were a cloudburst. Surely he could not expect us to go on if that happened. A moment later he looked up anxiously as well.

'Shall I row for a while?' I said at last.

'If you want.'

We swapped places. I was glad that he had scripted it – I had a chance to warm up. It was not very successful however; I had only rowed twice before and we had to break from the set dialogue for a while so that he could explain how I should do it. Eventually I found the knack, rowed for a few minutes, then resumed the script.

'Tell me about her,' I said.

'Who?'

'Your wife.'

He shifted uneasily in his seat. 'What do you want to know?'

'What was she like?'

He smiled. 'In what way?'

'Do I remind you of her?' I tried to make it sound casual. He considered the question. 'A bit. Sometimes.'

'When?'

'When you're thinking.' He eased back more comfortably again. 'When you're thinking you twitch your mouth in the same way as she did.'

After I had read the script I had decided to develop the mannerism. 'Any other times?' I asked.

'Yes, when you're angry. There's the same look in your eyes.'

I smiled wanly. 'How about when I kiss you?'

He sat forward uneasily again. 'What are you trying to get at, Juliet?'

'Nothing special, I'm just interested that's all.''

'I don't believe you.' He put his hands over mine to stop me rowing. The boat glided on, slowing. I felt a twinge of nervous curiosity again, wondering how he would say his next line. 'You think I'm trying to recapture the past, don't you?' I did not reply. 'Don't you?' he repeated. He had a dead-pan expression on his face.

'Perhaps. It's just occurred to me.'

'Well I'm not.' He stared at me hard. 'You cannot bring back the past. Ever.'

'Not even when I kiss you?' My voice was weak.

'No, not even then.' He paused and looked away. 'You should know that with a name like yours.'

'Juliet?'

He removed his hands from mine and sat back again. 'Yes.

Romeo couldn't rouse her with a kiss, could he?' His eyes twinkled.

'Very clever.'

'But true.'

And then as if to prove the point obscurely, he leant forward once more and kissed me suddenly, unscripted. It was not passionate in any way, just a quick brush of the lips to rub the joke in. It caught me completely by surprise, threw me off track for a moment. I had that sense again of being played with; his manoeuvring to always keep one step ahead. I was not sure how to react.

He broke the mood immediately, looking suddenly at his watch and making to stand up.

'We'd better head back now or I'll be late for my meeting. Shall I row again?'

I nodded and we changed places.

As we rowed back to the boathouse he questioned me about the new production I was to be in shortly, but the dialogue had no importance – it was clearly just a filler, just as it was when it was my turn to ask him about his meeting; there was no ambiguity in the lines and he tackled his without much enthusiasm. After we had climbed out of the boat, we began strolling back down the Serpentine Road. We did not speak. I was grateful for the silence he had scripted – we walked arm-in-arm as naturally as any lovers might in the direction of the Bandstand where the last section of the script was due to take place, and where we were to part.

It felt right somehow. The simple fact that we had kissed and said the words we'd been scripted to say would have made it unnatural to do anything else – even though it was an acted love, there was still a bond of some kind: acting love meant one felt its ghost; it seemed the ritual of the game was enough to stir it.

And again, as Juliet had said, the acting increased one's awareness of what was happening. I could feel a slight tenseness in his grip, knew he was apprehensive about that last scene approaching. There was that peculiar sensation that I'd felt earlier as well – of all around me come alive: the trees, the birds, the pressure of his hand on my back, the feel of his coat beneath my fingers.

I was just about to break the silence, to say something about a woman who'd passed us, when he suddenly stopped stock still. He was staring in front of him, eyes fixed on a figure approaching in the distance. Immediately, he muttered something, then pulled me to the right down the path past the cafeteria, the Dell dipping away on the other side. I had to respond, improvise something. In the end I could only think of what was natural.

'What's wrong,' I asked.

He looked panicky, just as I must have looked at those first encounters. 'It's just someone I know—I want to avoid him.'

'From the university?' I asked lightly.

'No . . . well, someone from the conference I'm going to, actually.'

Suddenly I felt a desire to get back at him: throw him on to the defensive as he had done to me so often. I felt I had a lever.

'Would it be such a scandal?' I said.

He was floundering, patently worried that I was about to blow the whole set-up. He searched desperately for something to say. I let him stew a moment longer, then had to rescue him.

'What would he say if he saw you with a 21-year-old drama student?'

'Exactly.' He looked relieved.

'Couldn't you say I was your daughter or something?'

'Er . . . no . . . he knows Sally.'

'Ah, a pity.'

He glanced at me and I winked. 'It would have been nice to see how good an actress I really am.'

He glanced at me and I winked. 'It would have been nice to see how good an actress I really am.'

'I don't think that's necessary,' he said pointedly. It was an admission of defeat—his first. I felt a delicious sense of triumph: I had been ahead of him, controlling the game as I always liked to. I had a premonition of other such scenes; but when and for what reason?

I did not pursue it any further. We circled round the Dell and went back to the Serpentine Road. Whoever it was he'd seen was no longer around and we wandered along to the Bandstand, the point we'd started from, but did not sit down. There were many more people now; despite the weather the park had filled up over the lunch hour: office-workers out for a breath of fresh air, one or two steadily munching sandwiches. Fox walked us to a spot where we would not be heard beneath a tree behind the Bandstand. I felt my excitement mounting again, strangely eager to get the next part done.

At last he turned to me. 'Well, I'm sorry Juliet. It's 1.30. I'll have to move.'

I looked at him steadily. It was Juliet's now-or-never.

'Paul?' My voice was quiet.

'Yes?'

'When are we going to sleep together?'

I had not been sure if he would feign shock. In the event he didn't, but simply looked at me unblinkingly.

'We are going to sleep together, aren't we?'

Still he did not reply.

'You do want to, don't you?' I made myself sound uncertain, hurt.

'Don't be silly.'

'It's not.'

'I didn't mean that—of course I want to sleep with you.'

'Well?'

He put his hands up to my shoulders and regarded me slowly, but did not answer.

I went on nervously. ' . . . We could go back to my flat now if you wanted . . . the others wouldn't be there . . . there'll be . . . '

He shook his head almost dejectedly.

'Why not?' I couldn't tell if he was really nervous or just pretending. 'What was it you said that first time on the train: "Quick now, here, now—always. Ridiculous the waste sad time—" Isn't that right?'

'Yes.'

'Well, surely you could miss one boring old meeting?'

He smiled weakly; dropped his hands. 'I'm not quite sure that's what Eliot meant,' he said.

I looked down at the ground, feigning injury. Had Juliet really begged? It was just conceivable. Possibly she thought he was just nervous – the age difference, a rush of guilt? There was a long silence; a young smartly-dressed executive passed by close, then Fox spoke.

'It's not right like this, Juliet. You must understand. It's not that I don't want to – it's just that . . . '

Words failed him, he seemed to lose courage suddenly.

'Jesus! This is like some spotty adolescent's love-scene. I thought I'd finished with all that.'

He seemed to come to a decision. He began slowly. 'Listen . . . I've got to come up to the City again in about a fortnight and I'll have to stop the night. If I book a room for us . . . ' Again his courage left him. 'Oh, this is crazy.'

'No it's not.'

He glanced at me and then away once more as if embarrassed.

'Well . . . if I book a room for us at a hotel, maybe . . . it'll give you time to decide if you're really sure you want to.' He seemed relieved to have found a way out.

'I don't need time, Paul. Christ, it's natural isn't it? Lovers do go to bed you know.' He nodded and looked at me, but did not speak. 'Still, if that's the way you want it . . . '

'Well, it would give *me* time to think then.'

I shrugged. 'I don't feel terribly complimented.'

'I'm sorry, I didn't mean it like that.'

'No,' I said flatly. There was a silence. He was running his hand through his hair as if he was witnessing a death not this offer of love-making. I went on: 'My God, how did we ever get like this? It's all so heavy.'

'Yes.'

Another silence.

I was meant to break the mood. 'Look, we'll do it your way then. You'll phone me?'

'Yes.'

'Promise?'

'I promise.'

'Well, you'd better get along to your meeting.' I tried a smile.

He nodded once more, then did not know how to finish. I leant up to him and kissed him briefly.

'Go on then.'

'Right.'

'But make sure you call me.'

'I will.'

He kissed me then. There were goodbyes. The next moment he had turned and was striding away towards Hyde Park Corner. He stopped once to wave, then hurried out through the gate. A crazy, ponderous, theatrical parting.

I stood there for a while still watching after he had disappeared from sight, trying to work out exactly what I'd promised, then decided to sit down and smoke and let the beating of my heart subside.

It had been a faultless performance, of that I was certain. I felt exhausted, thrilled, almost drunk. But what had happened? What exactly had I accepted; what exactly had I offered? I knew that things had changed since those first two scripts. I had gone into them offering sex and nothing more. Now it was no longer so straightforward. What had started in the train had a life of its own now: a beginning, a middle and an end. This slow progression to the climax had begun the moment that I'd seen the advert, and with a strange helpless sense of fear I realized I could not control it. The wind bit suddenly through my jacket and I shivered. There would be one more script, I was sure of that. Set at a hotel. Weakly, reluctantly, wishing that I could say no, I knew in my heart that I would do it.

Fourteen

Over the next couple of days, yet again, my feelings changed. As that parting moved further and further away into the past and the melodrama of those moments faded I came gradually back down to earth. Yes, there would be another script of course, but what was required of me was really nothing special: it was simply my business, the area of the acting profession where I was expert. It had been a long time getting to this point, entertaining admittedly, and very lucrative, but in the end what was the difference between this and the usual performance I put on for clients? We would do it to directions – sex on stage – so what? It happened every single day. I would be able to handle it without any trouble, it would not demand much, and at the same time I suspected that I might well enjoy it, get the very kick from the experience that I had been looking for in the first place. I had no trouble sleeping, no fears about what was required; if anything I felt a minor sense of anti-climax. I resigned myself to waiting for the script to come and tried to think about other matters.

It came three days later. I can only say it was not at all what I'd expected.

The first thing, and only a minor point in a sense, was that the envelope was much thinner than I'd been anticipating. I had assumed that this would be the big one: the whole assignment had been building up to this – it was sure to be the longest. It wasn't.

There was a cheque again – £300, a letter; but I looked first at the script. It was only five or six pages long. My eye was caught immediately by what was typed right at the top – 'Scene: A Coffee-Bar'. I could not believe it. A coffee-bar! The old fool had chickened out. I dropped the script and turned straight to the letter.

Dear Ms Rivers,
    Thank you for coming to the Park. You were magnificent.
    I enclose a much shorter script this time which again I would like you to perform.
    Having already arranged their meeting at the hotel, Paul has now unexpectedly telephoned Juliet saying that he has had to come up to London on some urgent business. He asks her if she can meet him that lunchtime for a short while and they agree to meet in a coffee-bar.
    Could you come to Alessandro's on Oxford Street at 12.00 next Wednesday, July 2nd. I will be already sitting at one of the tables. The same clothes that you wore to the Park will be appropriate.
    I realize that this gives you very little notice and if you find this date is impossible, could you please telephone the magazine and leave a message for Box 14.
    I enclose you cheque.
                                    Yours,
                                    Paul Fox

I put the letter down a little disappointedly. He must have decided, I concluded, to call the night off altogether.

I went back to the script and read it through. When I had finished I said quietly, but aloud: 'You bastard, Fox.' Juliet had been exactly right – she'd said as much before me.

July 2nd was the following Wednesday so I did not have very long. Over that weekend the heat-wave returned with a blistering vehemence, and it was hard to find the energy to do anything very much. Nevertheless, I did do two things: I learnt the script and bought another copy of *Nevermore*, the book I'd been given to read on the train on that very first occasion.

I decided to have a look at the book for a number of reasons. Each time a script had finished I'd been reminded of the ending of that book – the 'You will come, won't you?' seemed to be mirrored in each of our partings. In addition to that both Paul and Juliet kept quoting that epigraph – there was a reference to it yet again in the script I was presently learning – and I thought that if I read the novel right through it might throw some light on what we were doing. Of course I'd already got the gist of what they meant but I thought it might give me a proper explanation.

The book was quite simply dissatisfying, there is no other way to describe it. The action took place on a Greek island and centred on two married couples who met in the hotel where they were staying for their summer holidays. The pace of the book was slow at first; long, involved but very evocative descriptions of the scenery and setting: the harbours and beaches, the bars and restaurants, the general holiday atmosphere. There was a sense that all was timeless – somehow you felt that the same wizened Greeks who went about their unhurried business in that village, fishing or herding goats or just sitting stolidly in the cafés, might have been there a century before; they were unchanging; silent wry observers of the absurdities that went on around them. Into this setting came the intruders from England – the two couples on their annual fortnight of escapism. Their flight out was described in detail – the headlong dash by plane had hurtled them, not only out of their country and the usual humdrum existence they shared, but out of the normal march of time as well; here new rules applied – or perhaps there were no rules at all.

At first the encounters between the couples were all very low-key. For the first couple of days or so they avoided one another with determination: 'I thought we'd come here to get away from other English people!' one of them, Mark, said irritatedly to his wife on the beach one morning. But it did not last long. Common politeness meant that they had to acknowledge the others' presence and very soon Mark was forced to admit that they weren't 'as objectionable as the usual brand of tourist one encounters from one's country'.

They began to meet accidentally – on the beach, on walks, in the tavernas where they went to eat in the evenings. Gradually the early indignation that each couple had felt on finding others trespassing in their haven turned to pleasure: they were on the same wavelength – in fact this fresh, unexpected company began to enliven their holidays. By the end of that first week they had started to arrange the meetings: going to the beach together, a trip inland to see the mountains, while in the evenings they chose to eat and drink together, sitting long into the night on the hotel terrace.

Slowly, two of the four – Mark from one couple and Sarah from the other – developed a teasing, flirty kind of relationship. It was not meant seriously; both had strong marriages and both regarded the attraction they felt for the other as nothing more than light amusement, but the magical atmosphere of the island imperceptibly tampered with their feelings. It was indeed an escape, this trip: the holiday was a suspended moment in which anything could happen; the locks had stopped, breath was held, and the usual code of conduct mysteriously disappeared. The flirting turned to deeper feelings. Yet neither felt this was being unfaithful – the island did not seem to exist in the same reality – and they began to conspire to meet, devising methods by which they would be alone as if by accident: swimming at the same time, being the first down to breakfast, leaving beachwear or cameras at the hotel so that they would have the opportunity of walking back together.

As the story moved on the pace increased: clearly the reader was being prepared for a massive climax. The moments that the couple snatched together became frighteningly intense, all they felt for one another had to be concentrated into the briefest minutes; the affair was packed with sudden melodramatic leaps of passion. Soon Mark and Sarah realized that they were sure to be discovered – they were suspected: dubious sidelong glances passed between the spouses; Mark's wife suggested one night that they should eat somewhere on their own for a change. 'We don't want to bore the others, they must be getting sick of the sight of us,' she announced, showing rather too obviously that she was jealous. But the affair continued – dangerously now; each brief encounter carried out in nervous whispers, each excuse made to be alone together more painfully suspicious.

Then the real world intruded. Suddenly the end of the holiday was only three days away, the return to reality became closer and closer with every second and still the affair had not been consummated. Unbelievably two days were left. Then one. If they were ever to finish what they had started it had to be that final night. It was an enormous risk, yet they did not question whether they should do it, but whether it was at all practical – they would have to sneak from their beds in the small hours and trust to God that the others did not wake, then at last make love down at the beach.

And that, cruelly, was where the book finished. Having taken you to this point, teetering on the edge of your fulfilment, the novel ended. You never knew if they went through with it or not, you were left hanging on that final line I'd already read, 'You will come, won't you?', suspended in the fiction, never to know, any guess you made quite pointless. As Juliet had said back in that very first script, it was fantastically frustrating – in all it senses.

I did not have much time to think about the novel – but I did not find what I'd hoped: clues about my role. There were some senses in which it was similar – the intensity of the moments snatched together was comparable to our scripted meetings, and there was the same artificial quality to it all. But I was confused. The book was no apparently advocating adultery – that was not the issue; it was more about concluding things, not leaving life unlived. Mark and Sarah's frustration was exactly mine – I suspected that the writer had played some elaborate trick on me, that it was some practical joke he'd played throughout: leading me on and then destroying the ending. His final laugh was to leave you on the island.

It gave me, at that time barely even faint, the first glimmer of an idea. I had a lesson for Mr Paul Fox.

Fifteen

I was a little late to the coffee-bar that Wednesday morning. This time I did not bother to go there early to see him arrive. By then I knew there was nothing to learn from that; I was no longer interested to see which direction he came from – if he wanted to appear out of the blue in the way he did, that was fine by me. Instead I thought that I would keep him waiting, slightly pre-empt Juliet in trying to hurt him, the tiniest hint of a rebellion.

It was a small Italian café. I glanced quickly through the window as I approached but did not see him, then walked in. There was a long self-service counter stretching from the doorway, the tables all at the back partitioned off from one another by hanging plants and wrought-iron decorations so that little snugs were formed where customers would be relatively private. In the centre three or four circular tables were visible with a few couples grouped around them, but I guessed I would find him in one of the snugs – it would better suit his plan for an undisturbed, intimate conversation.

Supposedly eager to see him I swept straight past the

counter. I was still intent on playing the part as he wanted, with only minor variations. The directions at the beginning of the script said that Juliet was excited and had been pleased by the sudden, unexpected phone-call.

He was where I had guessed he would be: in the farthest snug from the entrance, back to me as I approached, slowly stirring a cup of coffee. He was dressed in a suit; very serious as was appropriate. I took a breath and then swung round beside him with my greeting.

'Hi there!'

He looked up with the strained smile that I was expecting. I leant down to kiss him, but he offered only his cheek.

'Hello Juliet,' he said quietly.

'Hey, what's wrong with you?'

'Nothing. Come and sit down.'

I observed him for a moment as he looked away from me, pushing his coffee to the side as though he no longer wanted it. He was putting on a good performance, better even than I'd expected. I took off my coat, tossed it on to the long bench seat and sat down opposite him, then leant forward, elbows on the table, resting my chin in my hands as close to his face as I could stretch. I whispered teasingly.

'Was it the kiss? Did I embarrass you?'

'No.'

'I don't believe you.'

I leant further across in an attempt to kiss him again but he bent away from me.

'All right, yes, I was embarrassed.' He said it quietly but with a hint of petulance, and yet I knew that the reason he had given was not the truth; it was clearly scripted so that the subject could be dropped.

'Fuddy-duddy,' I said. 'Anyway it's lovely to see you.'

'Yes.'

'Well, you don't sound very keen.'

'I am, Juliet.' He squirmed a little in his seat. 'Look, what do you want to drink? A coffee?

'Yes, a capuchino,' I answered, sounding piqued.

He got up without a word and went to get the drink straightaway. While he was gone I took a packet of cigarettes from my bag and lit one. It had not been scripted; it was totally insignificant, except, I suppose, that it was my second tiny act of rebellion. When he returned, only a few moments later, carrying the coffee, I could tell that he had immediately noticed . for he checked his step. I spoke before he could think of some carefully-worded reminder; defiantly, intending to provoke him.

'Yes, I've started again I'm afraid, Paul.' I leered at him slightly.

There was a flash of anger in his eyes. 'You're very weak,' he replied, choosing his words. He put the coffee down in front of me, slopping some into the saucer as he did so. In a sense I had declared war and I saw that he realized it, but he did not pursue the matter. There was a brief silence, then I resumed the script.

'Why didn't you say last time that you'd be coming up today?'

'I didn't know until the last minute. It's . . . it's an emergency meeting.'

I nodded. 'And you've only got an hour again, I suppose.'

'Yes, I'm afraid so.'

'Jesus!'

He did not accept the challenge, he let the word hang in the air and began stirring his coffee again. I went on.

'Well, have you decided?' I allowed a trace of sarcasm to creep into my voice – Juliet already suspected. He was fingering his ring, not knowing how to broach the subject. At last he started.

'Juliet, I called you because I thought we ought to have a talk.'

'You don't want to go through with it, do you? You've decided?'

'No . . . it's not that.'

'What is it then? Christ, you don't make me feel very desirable, you know.'

He looked up. 'I've lied to you.' he said slowly.

I let my mouth fall open, faking consternation. 'What do you mean?'

'I am married, Juliet. I'm sorry. Mary isn't dead – I lied.'

I expelled a breath gently. The script directed me not to answer immediately, but to sit in stunned silence for a while. He was looking down at his coffee-cup, holding himself almost rigid, only his lips moving as he tensed and relaxed them. I felt lost suddenly, my rehearsals useless, not knowing how to utter the next line. I had planned to swear at him, to break from the script, but now I sensed Juliet's line was right.

'I see,' I said at last, quietly but with bitterness.

He shook his head. 'I'm sorry.'

'Oh for God's sake don't say you're sorry. It's pathetic.'

'I'm . . . ' He cut himself short, then looked down again.

I sighed. He had closed his eyes now and was slowly kneading his forehead in a way that instantly reminded me of my father with his 'migraine'. We'd had to creep silently in and out of a darkened room at home while he suffered with the nasty affliction; the shock comparison caught me unawares and a stab of true bitterness twisted inside me. This man was every bit as hypocritical as he, and on that instant I determined that I would get even.

I stabbed my cigarette out with one savage prod and took a sip of the coffee he'd brought, still too hot.

'Well that's it then, isn't it,' I said. He did not reply but gave a little nod. 'So much for our wonderful night of passion.'

He did not take it up. At that point according to the script I was supposed to start to cry but it didn't feel right for some reason – I certainly didn't want to and I sensed that Juliet would not have either; he was cheating. I took another scalding sip instead.

'My God, this is just like something from a play. All these people sitting around listening to our corny little tale of romance.' This was another joke of his, I guessed. 'It's incredible. I never thought it would happen to me.'

He looked up blearily and undid his collar.

'Just tell me why,' I whined. 'Why did you have to lie to me?'

He gestured desperately. From the front of the café we heard an argument start between the owner and his wife mirroring ours a moment earlier. The woman banged down a pile of plates and slammed the door to the kitchen as she marched out. Fox at last found some words.

'I never thought it would go this far.'

I snorted. There was another silence. The next part I was unsure about, I was not happy about the change of mood.

'I wouldn't have minded,' I said.

'What did you say?'

'I wouldn't have minded,' I repeated.

'But you said – '

'You didn't believe that did you?'

'Of course, why not?'

'My God, I though I was supposed to be naïve.'

He screwed his face up, feigning utter incomprehension. 'You mean to say it wouldn't have made any difference to you at all?' A slick of his hair fell across his forehead and he brushed it back.

'No, of course not. I think I was secretly hoping that you were married.'

He shook his head wearily. 'My goodness, now *I* don't understand.'

'Look Paul,' I said, 'I know it'll sound a bit stupid, but it was more fun that way. You know – having an affair with a married man, all that business.' I made an explaining gesture with my hand, but the lines did not come out well – even in rehearsals I had not felt happy with them. He gave a short, snorting laugh.

'Don't you see?' I went on, 'It seemed exciting. It wasn't the usual dreary old affair. The secret meetings, an hour stolen here and there, not being able to phone you. You being so much older . . . all the clichés . . . '

He was staring at me, his wide eyes trying to penetrate mine.

'So you knew I was lying?'

'I think so, yes.'

He shook his head again and stared at his coffee. I lit a cigarette, watching him carefully, knowi..g exactly what he was about to say. He pushed the sugar bowl around with the tips of his fingers. It really was a superb display of bewilderment. It was impossible to believe that he had scripted the whole thing, that the scene was just play-acting, and I felt helpless suddenly, my little gestures of rebellion quite meaningless. How helpless Juliet must have been as well against this intriguer, totally out of her depth. He looked up now, coming to a decision.

'So what's different now then?' he said.

I returned his gaze, considering momentarily breaking from the script again and stopping him from getting away with any more. But no, I would wait. There would be a better opportunity.

I tried to sound confused. 'Oh, I don't know,' I said.

'You must have wanted me to lie. You must have wanted me to keep up the widower-pretence. Don't you see that?'

I nodded bleakly.

'So what's different?' His voice was insistent. 'Why can't we go on?'

'I can't explain.' I shifted uncomfortably in my seat, wondering if I would regret this.

'I know I lied, but if you wanted me to, it can't make any difference.'

'You've spoilt it.'

'I don't understand.'

'It's not the same. It's not a game any longer.'

'That's stupid – it can be.' He looked at me directly. 'Of course it can be – if we want it to.'

'It wouldn't ever be the same.'

He hesitated, then leant across the table almost whispering. 'Look, why don't we go ahead as before. I *do* have to come up next week for a couple of days. Why don't you come to the hotel as we arranged.' He sounded like a criminal conspiring with me in a murder-plot. I did not answer. 'Remember those lines?'

'Which?'

'You said them yourself – "Quick now –"'

'All right, there's no need to go on.'

'There are no second chances, you know.' He stretched a

hand across and covered mine carefully, the eyes imploring now. 'I really do want to make love to you, Juliet. Say yes.'

I snatched my hand away. 'This is crazy,' I said. 'Last time it was me trying to get you to agree.'

'Well?'

'We've had all this before.'

'So what?'

'I don't know.' I felt Juliet – or myself – slipping, needing a breathing-space. 'I want more time to think about it. Yes, I want more time to think about it. That's fair, isn't it? That's what you did to me last time.' He smiled. 'Well, it is, isn't it?'

He raised his eyebrows and nodded. 'Yes, I suppose it is.'

I put my hands on the table with a kind of finality, as if to convince myself that I had made the correct decision.

'Yes, we'll leave it like that – I might come and I might not.'

'You won't tell me in advance?' There was a hint of excitement in his voice.

'No, I won't.' I enjoyed the moment. 'You'll just have to wait and see.'

He looked across to the other tables where a middle-aged couple were just leaving. They gave us a scathing look, clearly having overheard the conversation. Fox turned back to me and spoke. There was an added ambiguity.

'Well, I suppose I deserved it really.'

'Yes Paul, you did,' I said. I lifted the cup of coffee to my lips, still holding his gaze, and took a long drink. I could feel a smile teasing at my lips, feeling that I had cornered him with my words, forgetting for an instant that he had scripted it; he was not being set up at all – quite the reverse.

There were only a few lines of the dialogue left. I finished my coffee and replaced the cup.

'Do you want another?' he asked.

'No, I don't think so, thank you.'

'Are you sure?'

'Yes . . . I think I'll go now.'

'I've got another half-hour.' It was said as a question.

'I think I'd rather go.'

'As you wish.' He was only being polite. Even if I had been Juliet I suspect he would still have wanted me to go. 'So this might be the last time that I see you,' he said flatly.

'Yes, it might.'

'We'd better say goodbye then.'

I decided to sound firm, quite unrepentant. 'Goodbye,' I said.

'Is that all?'

He held my eyes for a moment longer, deciding whether to protest or not, then finally came down against it.

'I'll be waiting, Juliet.'

'Good,' I said.

The directions for my departure were very clear. I was to lean across the table, kiss him once on the lips, then stand immediately. I did exactly as I'd been directed; he made no attempted to change it; I marched straight out of the café with a last, ambiguous, 'See you!'

I did not wait around to see him leave, I made no attempt to see which way he would go. But as I hurried to the Underground that final line hung in my mind, and I began to wonder seriously whether like that book I had been fooled; perhaps, after all, this was the ending.

Sixteen

Later that day I went to the Job Centre. It was an on-the-spot decision: I'd come to the end. I didn't examine my motives, nor did I have anything particularly in mind; I just wanted a full-time job – work that would be enough to support me without having to resort to clients again.

I hadn't given any thought either to the kind of questions they might ask. I was caught out by a number. The first was: what had I been doing over the previous two years? I told them: part-time typing, then found I had to explain how I'd managed to live on that alone. My story was not so far from the truth. I said I'd been living with someone – off his earnings largely – but that now we'd broken up. The interviewer didn't see the irony and clearly thought my fit of laughter a little perverse.

When he asked about the future, I can't explain what happened. What sort of thing was I looking for, he inquired. Did I want to retrain? On the spur of the moment I thought of nursing, he wrote it down and said he'd look into it. As for the meantime – would I accept more typing? I shrugged and was lectured: I was lucky; there was some work for the following day – only a fortnight's fill-in for a girl who was on holiday, but these days one should be grateful. At least it was a start. I had made the break. He said he would contact me about the nursing 'in due course'.

As I left the building I tried to work out why I'd done it. It was not really the cash. Admittedly, I did need some: I'd not had anyone back at the flat for over a fortnight – with Fox and the scripts and my own private drama to think about I'd put the callers off. Of course, there were the cheques: I could always have used them – but I didn't want to. They were still in the bank, untouched; in some obscure fashion I was coming to regard the money as Sylvia's, not mine; they were immoral earnings that I refused to touch. So I was short of money – and yet it was not that.

Even that night I failed to analyse my reasons. I rang round all the clients who would not be compromized by a telephone-call and told them I was moving. I said I wasn't sure yet where I was going, but that I would contact them. Most of them made no comment – indeed, they seemed surprised that I was ringing, but one, cynical and perceptive as ever, asked me if I was 'retiring'. I said 'yes' and put the phone down, then went to watch television. I still didn't understand quite why I had done it. I simply felt tired, no longer interested in anything, bored with all around me, and most especially, with myself. It wasn't until Fox's final letter came that I at last admitted what had prompted my 'retirement'.

It arrived three days later; a thin, ordinary, letter-sized envelope. I put it on the table and just stared at it for a long while – knowing that I would read it, but somehow wanting to delay the moment, to torture myself. I remember noting how I felt, memorizing the whole situation, as if at some point in the future I would need to recall it.

Everything was still in the room, only the clock ticking. From the flat below I could hear the television and outside a youth shouting down the length of the street: I was reminded of that morning when I had lain in bed and listened to the sounds outside – muted, distant noises from another world. I felt the same now: alone, cut off from everything, both within time and yet outside it.

Eventually, without ever really making a conscious decision, I rose, went into the kitchen and returned to the table with a knife. I picked up the envelope, observed it with and odd disinterest, then slid the knife under the unglued part of the flap and slowly drew the blade through the fold. It made a rasping sound, shockingly loud in the silence of the room. I replaced the knife on the table and drew the contents from the envelope.

It was a single sheet of paper. No cheque, no script, just that single sheet of paper. It said quite simply:

The bar of the Carlton Hotel, Bayswater

9.15 July 9th

He hadn't even bothered to sign it.

I must have held it for almost five minutes – quite calm, showing no emotion. I did not really think about it, I did not need to – I understood it all in a flash. As soon as I read the note I knew why I had gone to the Job Centre. For the first time ever it was brought home to me what I was: a prostitute. I felt like a tart. Of course it had always hurt when I'd overheard a comment in the street or noticed the nod and laugh of smug men in pubs, but it had never cut deeply. Now I saw exactly what I was. And it had taken Fox to show me, his absurd little game, the pretence that I was not the very thing that I was. He did not simply want to use my body; he wanted very much more. It was not that he intended to sleep with me merely, he actually wanted *me*, my mind and body. He was going to use me – all I was – so I'd have nothing left. How many times had I acted with my body? Countless dozens – oh, it had been superb training for the role, but now more was required. He wanted me to act with my heart.

I picked up the envelope to reconfirm that there had been no cheque, then sat still a moment longer. At last, with careful deliberation, I folded his note and replaced it in the envelope. Next, I slowly stood, took it over to the drawer and slipped it in with all the others, each movement controlled and precise. Then I went across to the mirror and looked at my face. I was unfamiliar to myself. The eyes were too staring, too unblinking, too remote. My mouth was tightly-drawn and the lips were white. I felt a little afraid; when I tried to smile, to reacquaint myself, my whole face felt numbed as if I were wearing a face-pack. I turned away and then back, as if I hoped I might surprise myself. It made no difference. I felt strangely dissociated from my body, I felt I was being controlled by someone else. Time seemed to have ceased. It was as though I were outside it, existing neither in the present, nor the past, nor the future. I moved away, went up to the clock. It was just possible to make out the hands moving: it could only be the present. And yet I knew what would happen. It seemed somehow that it already had.

Seventeen

I closed the door behind me. There was a tiny click, the faintest clacking of the latch; an end and a beginning contained in that one moment. I smiled.

Outside it was still light. A burning sunset was glowing on the buildings, toasting the brickwork a vivid orange, and I thought: the Fire of London, eradicating the plague. There was no wind; it was midsummer; people were idling in the street.

I had not called a taxi; I walked steadily to the tube-station. I wanted to prolong each minute, to savour each unrepeatable second of that special evening. I felt drunk; both hilarious and serious, totally uninhibited. Ii crossed each corner without stopping, hardly caring to check if traffic were approaching. I was thinking: where is he now? Having dinner or getting dressed? Perhaps already seated in the bar? Whatever he was doing it did not matter. At 9.15, I knew, he would be waiting.

In the station, the machine issued the ticket with a heavy thud. I moved through the barrier, then stood inertly on the escalator. Going down, I had the sense of drowning: the platform level was moving up to meet me, the steps dissolving and disappearing. The metal grid had spiky teeth. I stepped over, felt the floor arrest me.

What followed I remember only episodically. I felt mesmerized. I recall staring at a poster. Then on the train, the carriage juddering at a station. A man was watching, the motor throbbing; its steady pulsation suddenly aroused me. I have no clear idea of arriving at Bayswater.

After that I was in a pub killing time. A greasy-faced man asked me pointedly for a light. I looked at my watch.

Then finally in the hotel. This I remember perfectly. I have a distinct recollection of standing before a mirror carefully arranging the hair-piece. I was thinking of Juliet's decision: working out what she had been feeling. Her voice was timid, tiny, like a bird-song. And she would stand with her arms just hanging limply.

Fox was at the bar, once again seated on a stool, with his back to me. He looked as if he had been there for some time. He was hunched up, weary, and swirling whisky around in a glass. I took in the setting. The carpet was a rich wine-red colour deepened by the orange wall-lamps which lit the room. The curtains were already drawn, heavy velveteen drapes, blotting out the summer evening. There was only one other couple, an elderly pair, quietly discussing in German some brochures they had open on their table. A middle-aged woman was sitting behind the bar at the far end, reading a magazine.

I walked silently over to Fox and stood behind him. He was absolutely still, as if he had sensed my presence and frozen, afraid of what might happen. I relaxed my arms, remembering that last-minute decision, and let them hang down by my sides, then took one final breath to compose myself. An eyelash was twitching at a lid, but I did not rub it. Strangely, I liked its teasing.

'Paul,' I whispered. 'It's me.'

He swung round, startled.

'I decided to come,' I said quietly.

He could not speak immediately. His eyes widened, then

clouded, as if this time, at last, he was not acting. Then he looked down.

'Thank God,' he said. 'I couldn't bear it.'

'Nor could I.'

He slowly nodded.

I went on instinctively, without rehearsals. 'Did you think you I wouldn't come?'

'Yes.'

'I nearly didn't.'

Again he nodded. He looked broken, almost helpless. There was no hint of scheming.

'When you left the coffee-bar you'd decided not to.' He said it as a statement.

'Was it obvious?'

'I was certain.'

'But you still came down here to wait?'

'Yes.'

We were silent for a moment.

'How long have you been here?'

He dropped his gaze. 'An hour . . . about.'

I examined his expression. He looked like an old man now, confessing; yet I felt no pity. I knew I was holding all the cards. I paused again, then reached down and took his hands. They were hot and swollen, shaking a little. I held them still, then squeezed them gently.

'Well, I'm here.'

His eyes melted, as if he were on the point of tears. He moved his lips to speak, but didn't. Momentarily I thought he had forgotten his lines, then remembered there were none. He simply did not know how to go on. I continued standing there, searching desperately for a sentence.

'Christ, I'm so nervous,' I said.

'So am I.'

We both grinned anxiously.

'Do you want a drink?' he asked.

'Yes, I think I'd better.'

'Wine?'

'No, something stronger – brandy, please.'

He turned away at once and called the barmaid over, clearly relieved to have a few moments' silence. I felt nervous too, what I had planned suddenly so difficult. The intensity of his reaction had completely thrown me. I had expected him to be more uncertain this time, but now I saw that all his poise and control had vanished, I suspected that what I had in mind might seem a rather hollow victory. He avoided my eyes as I settled on the stool beside him.

The barmaid handed him my glass and moved away, apparently with a lack of interest. He passed the glass across, then spoke, at last finding a voice.

'This week has been ghastly,' he said.

I haven't enjoyed it exactly.'

'I couldn't think of anything else – I felt like a sixteen-year-old again: lying awake at night, not being able to face any food.'

I smiled timidly. 'Me too.' I took a gulp of the brandy. It made me wince, the spirit eating into my throat.

He turned to me, looked as if he were about to speak, stopped, then started. 'Do you forgive me?' he asked haltingly.

His hand was on the bar. I covered it with mine and held his gaze. 'Wait and see,' I said.

His eyes flickered. I took another sip of the brandy. A wave of nausea rose in me as it reached my stomach and I realized I would not be able to finish the drink. I put the glass down.

'Paul?'

He turned again, anxious.

'Can we go upstairs? I don't think I want this after all.'

He seemed to flinch. It was almost as though he had not been mentally prepared for this, but now the moment had come, realized he would have to face it. He nodded slowly, almost gravely.

I faltered. 'Look, if – '

He broke in with sudden firmness. 'No, you go first. If we both go up together it'll look bad. I'll follow you up in five minutes. Here's the key.'

He reached into his pocket and handed it to me: a normal

Yale-type, but with a bulbous wooden number-tag attached, impossible to conceal. I noticed the German couple watching us out of the corner of their eyes; it must have looked even more like a pick-up than if we'd left together. I responded with a flash of provocativeness, leaning across to kiss him.

Don't be long,' I whispered.

He held my stare. 'Five minutes.'

I took his hand again and held it, then stood up. He gave a tiny nod of his head, almost imperceptible. I turned and left the bar.

As I walked back into the foyer the glow of the sunset, redder now, streamed in through the entrance, filling the hallway. I moved straight ahead, taking care not to glance at the reception-desk as I passed, and approached the foot of the staircase. Some new arrivals were gathered there and as I reached them they stood aside and their conversation ceased. I knew they were watching me. I climbed the stairs with studied precision, feeling their gaze on my back. My blouse prickled against my skin.

I reached the first landing and looked at the signs indicating the room-numbers: one to fifteen to the left, sixteen to twenty-two to the right. The outline of a finger pointed. I checked the key: seventeen. There was still time to turn back. I walked down the corridor. It was lit with a sickly light like the lower deck of a ship and as I moved forwards I felt myself sway against a wall as if it were indeed a boat, the whole place rolling in a heavy swell. I reached the door. I did not have to open it. He had given me this chance, another opportunity to back out. At once I saw that this was why he had done it: told me to go first — it was another test; not the pick-up business — he wanted total commitment.

The key sank easily into the lock. I turned it. There was a tiny click. The door swung open.

For a second I was afraid to look inside, then I moved through. The room too was suffused in red, the bed up against the back wall, facing the window, so that the deepening tones of the sunset fell across it. I leant against the door and closed it with my back, resting there against it, head on the wood. There was very little in the room – a simple set: a built-in cupboard, two chairs, a table, the hotel ashtray; nothing else. I could not see a case. Suddenly I thought: this is a trick. Like that first meeting, he'll stand me up. It was all some sick perverted joke: he was a woman-hater, Juliet had betrayed him – in this way he would avenge himself. The whole thing, the scripts, the money – just for this: the pleasure of imagining me up here, waiting for him, wanting him at last.

Or maybe not. A more horrible thought flashed through my mind: those things I'd considered before I'd seen him, the one who came up to my flat that night. I felt a tight knot in my stomach. I would not hear him in the corridor, he would enter with another key, no need to knock. He had a grudge against tarts, some obsessive mission to rid the world of us. What would he use? A knife? A stocking? No, stop. There was Juliet. Everything would be all right. I was playing the part of Juliet. The sickness receded, then suddenly surged back. Where was she now? Was this the act? He had murdered her as well and I was to act it out.

I started to turn to the door, then stopped. There was a sound. The echo of footfalls in the passage. They were coming closer. Stopping at the door. Then a tap. I did not move, just held my breath. Again the crazy beating of my heart. Another tap. I could feel it through my back. Silence. And then a nervous whisper.

'Juliet?' Again, 'Juliet?'

A thrill of fear went through me, arching down my back, finally knotting deep inside me. I felt weak. I wondered: had Juliet decided not?

There was a heavy sigh outside, a shuffling of feet, then the footsteps began to recede down the corridor.

Suddenly I knew it was not right. Whatever it was, it could not end like this. I would let him in. I would welcome it.

I span round, snatched at the lock and opened the door. He had reached the landing and was about to descend the stairs. His head was bowed.

I called out. 'Paul!'

He turned as if he could not believe it, his eyes wavering, trying to focus.

'Paul!' I repeated. 'I'm sorry – come here.'

From that moment we did not speak. He came slowly back down the corridor, hesitating slightly, and stopped beside me. I took his hand and led him into the room, then closed the door behind us. He was shaking minutely, a tiny quiver in his legs. At last I was totally in control.

For a few seconds I stood there watching him and smiled, waiting till the beating of my heart had slowed. The sun had dropped now and the glow was gradually fading, shadows stretching out across the room. I hesitated a moment longer, teasing him, then gently reached a hand up to his neck and pulled him to me. His lips were dry, trembling. I grazed them against mine, then licked them. There was a faint taste of whisky on his breath and his eyes were open. I pushed my tongue into his mouth and licked all around inside, but the tenseness in his jaws did not slacken. I drew away and looked at him again. The light in the room was failing quickly and his skin had a wax-like sheen. He was avoiding my eyes; his gaze was lowered to the floor. His arms were slack my his side. I thought: I will have to lead him, be the teacher.

I took one hand by the wrist and brought it slowly up to my breast, then pressed it there. He did not move. I covered his hand with mine and began to knead it. I massaged myself with his hand in deep rhythmical strokes, feeling a stiffening of my nipple as I did so. He was totally in my power, quite helpless, the perfect client.

At last he found the courage to return my gaze. His eyes were soft and watery now, begging for mercy, knowing that he could not control what he has started. Finally his other hand came up to my shoulder. I released my grip, but now he continued to massage me, slowly at first, then with gathering urgency. After a moment he drew me to him. This time the kiss was searching. He seemed suddenly frantic.

At that point I broke away. I took two short steps back and began to undo my blouse. He did not move, but watched me

167

drunkenly. I released each button slowly, slipped it from my arms and dropped it on a chair. I smiled, then crooked my arms behind my back to unclip the bra. He took a step towards me, uncertainly, and stopped. I unclasped it, let it fall from my shoulders. I felt a beautiful cooling relief to be free of all restriction; in that second supremely powerful. I stood quite still, watching him, knowing that if I snapped my fingers I could have him kneel before me, head bowed, pleading for forgiveness. A smile tugged at the corners of my lips again. I twisted my skirt round, unzipped it, and let it drop to the carpet. Still he was not moving, but simply gazing at me blearily as though he could not believe what was happening. I stepped out of my skirt, kicked off my sandals and put my hands to my briefs. Now I had to be swift. I removed them in one fluent action and stepped over to him. I smiled sweetly and touched his twitching erection through the fabric of his trousers. Then I undressed him. Quickly.

When I'd finished I allowed myself a second's study. He stood before me totally naked, white and nervous like a hospital patient awaiting surgery. His eyes looked helpless, yet still I felt no sympathy. I delayed no longer. I moved closer, reached down again to take him in my hand and squeezed gently. As I released him he grew harder and moaned but did not move. I gave a dainty smile, then swiftly drew my hands up his sides and down again. This time I toyed with him, teasing the tip and stretching back the skin, watching his expression closely all the while. There was a tremor. I leant forward to his ear and murmured, then put my hands up tos shoulders and began tracing them slowly down his body. As I reached his waist I knelt and drew my fingers round inside his legs. For a moment longer I carried on caressing, then took him in my lips and licked him. Momentarily he flinched, as if with pain, but after placed his hands upon my head. While I worked at him I felt his fingers begin to stir my hair. Ten seconds, no more; I could sense that he was ready. I eased up from my knees and moved across to the bed, leading him after, then lay down and pulled him to me.

For a second he made as if to climb beneath the covers. I stopped him and whispered: 'No, I want to see you naked.' He did not protest. He lowered himself down almost meekly, then lay there watching me. From then on I knew he would be obedient. I began my patter.

'Come closer,' I said and stretched across to meet him. 'Give me your hand. Put it here. Up and down my back. And bite my ear.' His eyes were closed. 'Don't be afraid,' I said. 'You can do it harder. And now between my legs. Oh, that's lovely. Does my wetness excite you?' His breathing had started to labour. 'Oh Paul, how I want you. Press hard up against me. You're so warm and hard. I want you so badly.' I felt him beginning to tremble. 'Do you want me to kiss you? Oh no, there's not time – I want you inside me.' I urged him nearer, but stopped him as he began to clamber over. 'No, I want to be astride you.' He had no chance to quarrel. I rolled him on to his back and climbed over his body. 'Here, let me guide you. God, that's so lovely. Sliding in deeply.' He squirmed, sensed a danger. 'Come on,' I said, 'go even deeper.'

I waited till he was was right up against the hilt, swelling me out, then thrust down on him, pressing myself harder still against the bone. He was both desperate and helpless. Inside I was aching, wanting to double up, yet pushing even deeper. His eyes were closed again. I knew the time had come. He couldn't stop.

I said: 'Was it like this that she did it?'

His eyes screwed up tighter. I went on.

'I don't think you heard me. Did she do it like this?'

His eyes opened. I grinned.

'No, don't go soft inside me. Was she on top or below you? Were her tits any bigger?'

I leant forward.

'Was her cunt any tighter? Did she moan much?'

Her jerked.

'Close your eyes if you want, you'll still have to hear. Hey, are you sure she wasn't blonder?'

I could tell he was close.

'Come on, quicker and deeper! Did you speak, Mr Fox? Didn't you say that you loved her?'

He tried to speak.

'Come on, one last effort! You know you can do it.'

I pinned down his arms.

'Should I speak? Should I say it? Those lines, Mr Fox? This is what you've paid for.'

He struggled.

'Did she say? . . . Did she say? . . . I'll bet . . . I'll bet it was . . . "Quick now . . . here . . . now . . . always – "'

Lonely and helpless, he pumped himself out inside me. I was trying to smile, but at the last moment failed. As I watched him writhe below me I was reminded of a baby. His face was so pained and so puffy and his fists tightly clenched. I rolled off and collapsed on to the pillow. Suddenly I felt I was going to cry. I tried to fight back the tears.

Eighteen

Fifteen minutes passed. We lay quite still, neither speaking nor moving. The darkness had begun to fill the room, a slow decay spreading down the walls, across the carpet, rolling up over our bodies. Slowly all was being covered, the chairs, the table, the silky bedspread rumpled beneath us; the colours all converging into greys and blacks. All was silent. Once there was the sound of someone padding quietly down the corridor behind our heads, then the distant opening and closing of a door, but it seemed a world away, as if it were occurring in a different lifetime. Only the numbness in the arm I had rolled on proved to me that I was living; it ached dully, yet I couldn't summon the will to move.

My head was twisted on the pillow so that I could see him. He lay on his back, corpse-like, staring wide-eyed at the ceiling; I studied his body with a mortician's detachment. Sixty years had not ignored him. I had not really noticed when he first was naked – he looked his age; there was no way that he could hide that. Little bags of skin sagged on his chest and there was the loose flabbiness of a paunch. Beneath, the hairs were totally white, his limp member lying there like some shrivelled rotting vegetable. His legs were hairless, almost shiny, their whiteness so deathly; all his limbs so still I thought of rigor mortis.

I felt that I had murdered him; I had not simply spoilt his moment, I had destroyed his dream. I wondered sickly how long he had lived on it. A year? Five years? Since the day it had happened at least – since Juliet had lain here in my place. Bitterly, I thought: could it really have been so special, so unforgettable as to warrant all this? Tonight I knew he would never forget, but there would never be any attempt to enact what had happened between us, no matter how far it receded into the past he would never regard it with that kind of sentimentality. For indeed that is what it was: a part of the past – that explosive moment we'd both witnessed already seemed strangely long ago. I could consider it distantly. The hunger I'd felt was all gone, the ache I'd suffered completely dead.

I tried to remember how I'd felt. I knew that I'd both wanted him and wished to destroy him, but now that my vengeance had been settled those urges did not seem quite real, they had died along with all the hate. My other hand still lay on his thigh where I had left it, but when I tried to move it those fingers too would not respond; I was quite numb. I thought of what they say of every sex-act: in a sense it is a little death. I wondered ruefully just who was dead.

At last a shiver shook me. The earlier warmth of the room had entirely dissipated now the sun had gone and I was forced to move. A voice inside me that I did not create, spoke. I surprised myself.

'Come on,' I said, 'let's get into bed.'

It sounded shockingly loud, almost a sacrilege to break the silence. He didn't answer. I moved my hand and this time it just tingled slightly. I gave his leg a gentle pat. His eyes flickered for a moment but he did not turn his head.

'Come on,' I said again and pulled myself up the bed. My tone was friendly rather than ordering and he did move then – not I think because he wanted to join me beneath the covers or because the cold had reached him, but rather because he could not bear to argue. We slipped between the smooth starched sheets, not touching, yet together in a sense.

It was a strangely beautiful moment lying there like that, letting time drift over us. It was the relief, that feeling that whatever had happened it was over; we had lived through something, we were survivors. There was a link – almost respect: as two war-veterans of opposing sides might reminisce with a kind of comradeship once the hate is spent.

Yet gradually, as we lay side by side and warmth returned, that moment also slipped. Explanations were required and I knew it was time to speak.

I said the first thing that came to me. I asked gently, 'Is she dead?'

The question hung in the room, settling down around us slowly, that first rule of his – of not asking questions – meaningless now that the last act had ended. He gave a small huff of ironic laughter and I realized suddenly the double-edged nature of the question.

'No,' he answered at last, then added as an afterthought: 'At least, I don't think so; I suppose it's possible.'

'You don't know what's happened to her?'

'No.'

I didn't comment but nodded gently, then lay there thinking; like him just gazing up, watching the shadows spread across the ceiling. We had spoken our first unstaged words and it felt odd. I recognized all of a sudden that we were complete strangers: I knew nothing of him, nor he anything of me. I was unsure of how to speak. There was a steady hum from somewhere down below us: an air-extractor perhaps.

'Christ, I could do with a cigarette,' I said.

He seemed to brighten a little. 'There are some in my jacket. I'll get them.'

'No, it's all right.'

I climbed out of the bed and hurried round to the chair on which I'd thrown his jacket when I had undressed him. He watched me passively as I stooped to the pocket, then followed me with his eyes as I returned to the bed. I felt strangely self-conscious, as if he were seeing me for the first time then, and not as a client, but as someone who shouldn't. I slipped back under the covers a little girlishly and tucked the sheet up under my armpits to hide my breasts.

I offered him the packet. 'Do you want one?'

He started to mouth 'No', then changed his mind and said 'All right.'

I leant over to the bedside table to get the ashtray and placed it on the covers between us. It seemed suddenly absurd: us lying there like that after what had gone before – and I remembered that moment in the taxi when we had sat so far apart before the kiss. I'm sure the same thought must have occurred to him as well, for he avoided my eyes as I lit his cigarette, then lay back rather stiffly. We were both silent for a while, the only sound our intermittent drawing on the cigarettes.

Finally I spoke once more. 'I suppose that's it, then?'

'What do you mean?' he said quietly.

His reply threw me. Perhaps I had not been quite certain with my question: it was not clear whether I was referring to the scripts or our relationship in general. I tried to play the question back at him.

'Did you mean us to go on after tonight?' I asked.

'Oh – no, that was it. The final script.'

I felt a tiny lump in my throat.

'Except there wasn't a script,' I said.

He gave that little huff again. 'Yes, except there wasn't one.'

I drew on my cigarette and it crackled noisily in the silence.

'What happened after this then?' I asked. I tried to be casual.

He looked at me as though he were slightly surprised. 'Nothing.'

I thought of Juliet momentarily. 'So after this, you ditched her, did you?'

He shook his head.

'She ditched you?' I said more gently.

'No.'

'What then?'

He seemed reluctant to answer at first, then apparently came to a decision. 'There was no night here,' he said flatly.

I was not sure how to react. It did not make sense. I stared at him incredulously. For a moment I wondered whether he could be acting once more, whether this was yet again a pose, but his eyes were unmoving and I sensed it was the truth.

'Do you mean –' I started.

'– There never was a night at the hotel.'

I paused 'She didn't come?' I asked carefully.

'No.'

'She did or she didn't?'

He moved his head and looked away. '*I* didn't,' he said. 'I didn't turn up. God only knows if she did or not.'

Instinctively I stretched out a hand beneath the covers and found his. He accepted it gratefully and stroked it gently. It wasn't so much that I felt a sudden sympathy for him, more that the idea of what had happened seemed so pitiable in itself. 'I'm sorry,' I said.

'I'm sorry too now,' he said with a trace of bitterness.

For a while I lay there recalling how I'd felt before I left the flat. I'd pictured him sitting in the bar waiting for me, and tried to decide which would hurt him most: what I'd done or not turning up. I'd finally chosen the former of course, but now I wondered if I might have been mistaken – not coming would probably have hit him harder. It was odd in any case, for now that all the bitterness and hatred had vaporized away I was no longer certain that I wanted to hurt him. I felt a kind of sorrow instead. I squeezed his hand momentarily and then released it.

'Do you want to tell me about it?' I asked gently. I had the sensation of slipping into another role: that of confidante or counsellor: the prostitute's other part.

He sighed. 'It's too complicated to explain.'

'Why don't you try?'

He shook his head wearily.

I looked at him. 'It's over now you know. I'm not out to get

175

you any more.' He held my gaze. 'Really,' I said.

He looked away again and drew deeply on his cigarette. 'What do you want to know?'

'Why you didn't come.'

He covered his face with his hands and pulled his fingers through his hair. 'Because I thought she wouldn't come.'

'Why?'

'Because I'd lied to her.'

'Just that?'

He reflected for a moment. 'Yes, just that.'

I could see it was not the truth, but experience told me not to press the point at this stage: he would come round to it in good time. I tried another tack.

'I thought the idea of all this was to get me to act out what Juliet had done so that you could relive it.'

He nodded. 'It was – up to a point.'

'But if she didn't come, how could I . . . ' I was going to say "re-enact" but at the very moment my lips moved to shape the sounds, the truth of it all suddenly came home to me. It was not a re-enactment at all – that was the whole point – it hadn't happened – I was acting it out to make it seem as though it had.

I turned to him quickly. He was looking at me, smiling weakly, not amused but embarrassed. His eyes were a little frightened too, as though he were afraid of how I would receive the idea.

'Do you understand now?' he said.

'I think I'm just beginning to,' I answered slowly. I waited a few moments but he did not accept the offer to speak. I went on: 'Let me get this right . . . you didn't sleep with Juliet?'

'No.'

'But you thought that if we acted it out, it would feel as though you had?'

He stubbed out his cigarette and closed his eyes. 'Yes.'

'You're mad.'

I did not mean it to be cruel – I said it without thinking. He slumped back to the pillow again, sighed quietly once more, then said: 'Yes, perhaps you're right.' It seemed quite possible that the thought had not occurred to him before.

I went back in my mind over all that happened – all the scripts he had written, all the time he must have spent, the money. It was over a thousand pounds. I couldn't imagine how anyone could have become so obsessed as to go to all those lengths, and for what – a fiction; to sleep with a girl by proxy?

'You must have been absolutely crazy about her,' I said quietly. I touched his arms to soften the words, but they injured me more than him. Again that twinge of jealousy I'd occasionally felt pricked at me – that someone should do all that for another girl – reach such dizzy heights of passion. I repeated it: 'You must razy.'

His reply surprised me. 'I wasn't though. I wasn't crazy about her.'

'You must have been.'

'You're wrong.' He shook his head wearily. 'I . . . '

'What?'

He answered as if he were explaining it more to himself than to me. 'I enjoyed being with her – but I wasn't "crazy" about her. Not obsessed.'

'What about all this then? Take a look at yourself.'

He was like a little boy frustrated at not being able to express himself. 'Yes of course, but that was later.'

'Why!' I exclaimed.

'Because it didn't finish! Don't you see? There was no *ending*. I didn't know whether she came or not.'

I thought suddenly of the novel. 'Like that book you gave me?' I said.

He glanced quickly at me, somehow furtive. 'What?'

'That book – *Nevermore* – don't you remember?'

He avoided my eyes. 'Yes.'

'You never get to know the ending.'

He looked away. 'Exactly. You can't stop there – it's unforgivable. There has to be an end to desire – it must be either killed or satisfied.'

We lay in silence. Suddenly it had sounded artificial; scripted again. I sensed that he'd said it before, worked it out already, perhaps even written it down somewhere. I guessed it was a posture, but didn't comment. Instead I said:

'So you planned all this – to satisfy it?'

He paused again. The other possibility occurred to me but I did not say it.

'I was just trying to finish something,' he said at last.

Again we lay in silence. I decided to drop the subject and looked over to the window. A light was switched on in the building opposite and I saw a figure pass briefly in front of the window and draw the curtains, then move away. Suddenly I thought I saw a weak link. I turned to him again.

'Couldn't you have found her and simply asked her if she'd come or not?'

'Do you think she would have answered?'

'Yes, why not?'

'With the truth?'

I put myself in Juliet's position for a second, then had to concede defeat. Either way, whether she had come or not, she would have been hurt. 'O.K.,' I said, 'I suppose you're right.'

He was silent for a moment, then added: 'Besides, I'd messed her around enough.'

I thought of saying something then did not bother. I could tell this was still not the whole story, but I knew that if I rushed him he might simply clam up. The barrier was embarrassment rather than bitterness and I was sure he would slowly overcome it. I gazed round the room for a while instead, trying to assimilate all the implications of what he'd told me. Somehow the absurdity of the whole idea seemed to be slipping away. The more I attempted to dismiss it, the more I found I was coming to believe it.

For a time I closed my eyes and tried to still the racing of my thoughts but it was impossible to empty my mind. I did not know this man and yet it did not feel strange lying there beside him; again I experienced that sensation of a bond. It was as if it had been some ordeal which we had both equally shared, a siege where hostage and captor develop a sympathy for one another. Somehow I felt that he had been as helpless as I, just as unable

178

to prevent himself from being the captor, as I had from being the captive. And in an inexplicable way I did not want it to end – despite what had happened I felt closer to him than anyone – indeed as a result of what had happened. I wondered a little glumly when he would expect me to get up and dress, and recalled momentarily the dreadful empty silence of the flat. Should I have left immediately, or would he make the first move? I spoke again quickly, afraid that a longer silence might provoke this. I went back to the lie he'd told Juliet.

'I still don't understand why you didn't think she would come. At the coffee-bar she said it didn't matter that you were married.' I turned to him. 'She said that was what she had been hoping all along.'

He gave me a pale kind of smile. 'She didn't say that. I made it up.'

'You what?'

'I invented it. She would never have said all that rubbish about having an affair with a married man. She wasn't like that.'

I remembered suddenly how uncomfortable those lines had sounded; I had sense they were not right, but now I was confused.

'What did she say then?'

'Nothing like that.' He looked strangely defensive, as someone who has got himself into a position he has been trying to avoid all along. He sighed again. 'I didn't tell her I was married.'

'Oh come on!'

'I told her something else.'

All of a sudden I'd had enough. This time I was certain I was being tricked.

'I'm not a complete fool, you know.'

'I know. This is the truth.'

'You don't seriously expect me to believe you, do you?'

He turned to fa me. 'Listen Sylvia,' he began.

I was sick of all the games. 'My name's not Sylvia,' I snapped. 'It's Shirley – you'd better call me that.'

He had leant over towards me to explain. His eyes were blank for a second then he fell back laughing.

Again I was caught off-guard. This was the reaction I'd least expected. 'What's so funny?' I said angrily.

He was helpless, face creased up.

'I don't see anything to laugh about.'

The bed shook with convulsions.

'Well?'

Finally he made an attempt to compose himself. He managed to stop shaking and tried to look serious. 'My name's not Paul Fox either,' he choked out.

'I didn't think it was. Big deal. What is it then?'

His eyes were watery still with the tears of amusement. I fixed his gaze. He became serious at last, the laughter finally dispelled. 'It's Fowler,' he said. 'Matthew Fowler.' He held the stare.

For a few seconds I could not place the name, where I had seen it. Then I remembered.

'You wrote the book?' I said.

'Yes.'

'*Nevermore?*'

'Yes.'

'Are you being serious?'

He nodded his head.

I continued looking at him, still unwilling to believe it, though suddenly a thousand previously ill-fitting pieces slotted into place. I examined his eyes though intuitively I knew this was the truth. I tried to watch them both at once and found that I could not, that I had to fix on one. It was peculiarly frustrating: I wanted to make absolutely certain and felt that if I could not watch them both at the same time I would never be able to confirm what he'd said for sure. Finally I had to give in. He had controlled the whole thing throughout and I realized at last that there was ultimately no point in fighting against him. I felt a smile beginning to break unwilled across my face, what resolve I had left crumbling. I grinned. He watched me carefully, then slowly retuthe grin. We did not move.

'I'm sorry,' he said quietly.

I sank gently back to the pillow. I spoke softly.

'Perhaps you'd better tell me what happened from the beginning.'

He eased down beside me and answered carefully. 'Yes, I suppose you do deserve some kind of explanation.'

'I think so.' I smiled.

A pause.

'It's quite a story,' he said hesitantly.

'I'm sitting comfortably.'

He threw me a quick glance to check that there was no sarcasm, then again fell silent for a moment. 'I don't know where to start.'

'You're the story-teller, not me.'

He grinned at that and closed his eyes. Somehow I got the impression that he did not know if he would be able to explain it to me, was not sure of himself now. Again that image came to me: the counsellor; the bed a psychologist's couch – my role was really just to lend an ear. He opened his eyes again and gazed up at the ceiling trying to find a way into the labyrinth he hast he began. 'It was just a game at first.' I glanced across. 'Truly – that was how it started.'

I turned back and grinned in the darkness. 'Don't tell me – you were travelling up to London by train when a girl walked into the carriage.'

'I know it sounds absurd – but yes, exactly. It was the classic situation, the start of a novel.'

'And she was reading *Nevermore?*'

He nodded. 'If she hadn't been reading the damn thing I would never have spoken to her.'

'But you couldn't resist asking her if she'd liked it?'

'No.'

'Why'

'Why not? Because I was bored – to amuse myself. I thought it would be totally harmless.'

'And had she liked it?'

'You know the script.'

'That was word-for-word with what she said?'

'As near as I can recall. I didn't tamper with anything until that final script.' He paused. Outside the hysterical screaming of a police-siren pierced the silence. We waited till the sound had died away.

'All right, go on,' I said.

He continued eagerly, clearly willing now to offer every detail. 'You must remember that at that stage I thought it couldn't possibly do any harm. When we reached Victoria we'd go our separate ways and she'd never know I was the author. It was stupid of course, I see that now, but it's always weird when you see your books being read or sitting on someone's shelf . . . ' His voice tailed off.

'O.K.,' I said. 'And then you found you liked her?'

'Yes – but it wasn't really that.'

'What was it then?'

'Well as I've said – the game. She forced me to assume a role – I had to invent all those details about lecturing at Sussex on the spur of the moment. It was like creating a character for one of my novels. I didn't do it to deceive her though, only so that she wouldn't be embarrassed.'

'All right, what happened then?'

He raised his eyebrows and gave a little huff again. 'That is when the real stupidity started. At the end of the journey I realized I'd enjoyed my little game and wondered if I could keep it up for another hour.'

'So you had a drink together.'

'Yes.'

'And didn't tell her who you were?'

'No. At the end I considered doing so, but then decided against it. It would have been too patronizing.'

I thought about it. What he said seemed credible enough – I decided to leave the script. 'All right, what about the Tate?'

'Ah, that was different.'

I leant over to get another cigarette. He shook his head as I offered him the packet.

'Why?' I said.

'The hand of Fate,' he smiled.

'It *was* an accident?'

'A total coincidence. I had no idea she would be there.'

'And why didn't you tell her then who you were?'

He halted for a moment and thought. 'I was going to say "for the same reasons", but that's not entirely true. You see, I was sure she was acting to an extent as well – putting on this super-enthusiastic show, playing at life. I suspected that she had an idea of who I was; there was a sort of twinkle in her eye as if she knew what was going on but would not spoil it all by giving the game away. Look at those scripts. I couldn't seriously believe she was interested in me for what I pretended to be: a 55-year-old French lecturer; it was absurd. I thought the game was very much a two-way thing.'

I took a long draw at my cigarette.

'And don't forget,' he went on, 'the whole time it was her that was forcing the pace, not me. She always made the first move – kissed me, asked me back, every step we took. I thought it might be amusing to see how far we could go like that; I was sure she must have seen a photograph of me in the interim; or simply guessed.'

I stared across at the window remembering that script – all the double entendres. It might just be the truth. 'And then you found she wasn't acting?'

'Well, not immediately. For a long time I still believed she knew who I was really – at the restaurant, the theatre, the meal she cooked.'

'Eh?'

'We missed out those scenes, do you remember? I didn't script them – they would have been too difficult to perform.'

I thought of all the problems there had been at the restaurant: that had been virtually impractical – any attempt to serve a meal and act at the same time would have ended in farce.

'It was only when we were at the park that time that I realized this character *was* her. She wasn't acting it. She was magical.'

Once again his words stabbed at my vanity – again I felt

jealous: that I had only acted Juliet, that I could not claim this for myself. Clearly he'd been more struck with her than he'd admitted earlier. I went on quickly.

'But you didn't tell her the truth then either?'

'I almost did – that business about being married. I was trying to test the ground. But the whole thing had gone too far by then; I'd had to invent so many details about Paul, lie so hard . . . I simply couldn't fact it.'

'So when she suggested sleeping together, you stalled for time?'

'I just wanted time to think, to work out what the best thing to do was. It wasn't a game by then. Do you understand – she meant it and I had duped her all along.'

I stubbed out my cigarette, though it was only half-smoked, and leant over to put the ashtray back.

'Right so we've got to the coffee-bar scene.' I felt an odd sense of impatience; that weird frustration when you think people won't explain quickly enough as they near the end of a story. 'You telephoned her and asked her to come to the coffee-bar.'

'Yes, I decided to come clean. I thought it would not be fair to go on without clearing the air – making sure that she had known all along.'

'And then you chickened out again?'

'No – I did tell her – that was what I changed in the script.'

'And had she known?'

He hesitated and rubbed his forehead once more. 'She had no idea,' he said quietly. 'It was a complete shock to her.'

I visualized the scene and tried to put myself in Juliet's position: finding that you had fallen in love with someone who did not truly exist, fictional character; she must have been totally humiliated. I muttered: 'The poor kid.'

He took a deep breath and looked over towards the window. The whole room felt chilled and empty. With his explanation of what had happened I had a strange sensation of something leaving me – the part of myself that was Juliet separating away like a spirit leaving the room. I shivered and stretched out for the reassurance of his hand once more. He accepted it but simply held it still, clearly lost in a world of his own.

I went on. 'So where you told me in the script you were married, you actually told her who you were?'

'Yes, that part was only in your script.'

'You didn't change anything else?'

'No – nothing.'

I paused. 'And are you married?'

He looked at me, surprised. 'Would it make any difference?'

I failed to recognize the line. 'I doubt it,' I said quickly.

He gave me a strange look. 'Well, I'm not.'

I paused again, then hurried on, embarrassed. 'And when you told her, she didn't lose her temper?'

'No.' He looked relieved to resume his story. 'She seemed to take it quite calmly – she even said a little later that she'd had an inkling I wasn't quite who I said I was.'

I nodded.

'But when she left it was on the same terms exactly as in our performance – she said I'd have to wait and see if she'd come or not. She wouldn't tell me.'

'She was taking her revenge?'

'I think so. I'm sure she had my book in mind – the ending of that – I was certain she never intended to 't come?'

'No.'

'And now you're not sure it was the right decision.'

He hesitated. 'I couldn't get it out of my mind. I thought there was a chance she might have forgiven me, that once she'd made her point she would show mercy – but it was too late by then – I hadn't gone.'

For a while we lay there silent, both of us turning over this unsolved ending in our minds. He held my hand, gently stroking his thumb across the back, but absently, not really considering me, but reflecting on all that had happened between them, all that might have been. I felt excluded; again that poisonous sneaking wish, that I were Juliet. I spoke simply to halt the dreaming.

185

'And then you planned all this.'

'Eventually.' The light went off finally in the room opposite. 'For a long time I thought I'd got over it, managed to put it to the back of my mind as a ridiculous episode never to be repeated. But it never settled. It preyed on my mind because of *Nevermore*. It was as if she had contrived the whole affair to teach me a lesson, plotted it to punish me for abdicating my responsibility towards the story. I was getting what I deserved: the same trick I'd pulled on my readers.'

I considered what he'd said. The moon was peeping in through the corner of the window now and a cool wash of milky light suffused the room.

'So you devised this scheme to provide an ending.'

'Yes,' he answered quietly.

We fell silent for a while and I began to wonder seriously for the first time whether Juliet would have come or not. Before he'd begun his explanations I'd been sure she had, now I was not so certain. The more I turned it over, the more I became intrigued.

Then he broke the spell. He started again, but this time with a trace of pomposity. 'It was partly an experiment as well – at least that's how liked to think of it. When you spend so much time in imaginary worlds manoeuvring characters this way and that, it sometimes becomes difficult to distinguish between what's fiction and what is not. There are extraordinary mental tricks you can play on yourself if you are only prepared to play them.'

I did not need him to remind me.

'I wanted to see if I could create a fictional world in reality.'

His theorizing grated suddenly. 'And did you?' I said. He did not notice my tone.

'Yes, I think so – but not the one I'd envisaged.'

I remembered my attempt to destroy him. 'Because I rebelled?'

'Exactly. The characters you create never do precisely what you want them to. They have a life of their own.'

I thought of my position once more and felt another stab of

bitterness. 'How observant of you,' I said sharply. This time he did notice, and it caught him unawares. He had not fully thought it through, was still really absorbed in his private fictions. I felt his eyes on me, a slightly perplexed frown. I went on: 'You didn't ever think of me, did you; what I might feel?'

He did not answer.

'You thought I was just a tart, didn't you?' I felt my anger rising again. 'That's right, isn't it?'

He was lost. 'I thought you wouldn't mind . . . '

'Because you paid me? Yes?'

Again he did not answer.

'Didn't it ever occur to you what I might feel acting out that part?'

He was speechless.

'You wrote your silly scripts to solve your problems – and I thought I was falling in love with you.'

'You what?'

I had surprised myself. 'Is that so fantastic. For a time I couldn't even tell who the hell I was. I almost came to think I was Juliet.'

'I'm sorry.'

'Don't say you're sorry, that's not the half of it.'

I'd sat up, leaning over him, the temper I thought was spent surging back once more. I was not really angry at him, it was just one last attempt to assert myself. 'I went and got a full-time job that afternoon. I'd decided I'd really had enough. I never wanted to be touched again, I never wanted a man to come near me again. I was through with it.'

His eyes were frightened, suddenly shocked at this outburst.

'I thought – just once more. One final time. And I planned exactly what I was going to do. I wanted to hurt you. Can you understand that? I wanted to really hurt you. I wanted to stick a knife in you. Jesus, I was almost ready to kill you. Believe me. But I knew you wouldn't suffer enough. I wanted to see some *pain* so I thought, what can I do that will really tear his heart apart? Completely destroy him. And it was so simple. I realized: Juliet. I'd destroy her instead.'

187

His eyes stared out at me from the gloom, horrified, remembering again what I had done, realizing perhaps for the first time that there was another person involved, not just he and Juliet. He looked so pathetic and defenceless, so completely astounded, that I felt suddenly weak.

'And I did destroy her, didn't I?' I said in desperation.

He didn't answer.

'Didn't I?' I repeated.

'Yes, you did.'

I didn't see the truth until that final moment. 'And that's exactly what you'd hoped for,' I choked. 'Exactly what you wanted!'

It was no good. All the bitterness had gone. I burst into tears and began to hammer on the pillow with my fists, mad with fury that I no longer detested him, incensed that I could not regenerate the hatred. I went berserk. For a moment he put an arm out tentatively, like a child nervously pushing a hand into a cage, but I immediately kicked out, completely unaware of whether I was hitting him, not caring if I did or not. He drew back to the other side waiting till the tantrum passed. For almost half a minute I thrashed around the bed, shouting and swearing, exhausting myself. Then it had to end. I burnt myself out. I lashed once more across the bed with one final despairing spasm, then fell still. It was a kind of exorcism.

He waited half a minute, then edged cautiously back across the bed and lay a hand on my shoulder. By then my wails had turned to sobs, the beating of my heart had slowed. It was over. There was no one else to turn to, so I turned to him. He held me still and gently stroked my back and head. The sobbing stopped, I sniffed. I felt him kiss my forehead, then my cheek. I had come to an end of all performance. I wanted to be close to someone, and no matter the reason, I was to him. We were inextricably linked – we had shared an experience which belonged to us alone. I felt him caressing my neck, then his fingers teasing at my ear. His hand started searching down my back. The room seemed changed; again that ghostly presence – the window painted with the pale blueness of the moonlight. There

188

were strange fuzzy sounds outside – the buzz of a scooter, the hum of the night. And he was kissing my eyes, licking away the salty tears, brushing my lips with his. I felt so naked up against him. I had a peculiar sensation – as if returning to earth from space – the touch of his skin and the warmth of his body so shockingly real. His hands smoother over the surfaces. All the times I'd lain like this and never felt the touch of the person.

I knew he was becoming aroused. I pressed myself against him and felt him growing hard again between us. I could feel the warmth of it nuzzling against my skin, searching up blindly in its effort to enter. I clasped him tighter and gently kissed him.

We made love like that, on our sides, slowly; out of forgiveness. It was silent and clinging and somehow almost innocent.

After, as we lay, his arm around me, floating weightlessly out to sleep, a forgotten idea reoccurred to me. I said quietly:

'I read your book you know.'

I could not see his smile in the darkness, but I sensed it.

'Did you like it?' he asked.

I considered his question. 'Not very much,' I answered.

He nodded slowly. 'The ending, I suppose?'

'Yes – it hasn't got one, has it?'

He shrugged. Briefly the room was light, the moon slipping out from behind a cloud and I came fully awake.

'What did happen really? Did they get together?' I asked.

I felt him stir. 'What did you say?'

'Did they get together? What happened?'

He began to laugh sleepily.

I turned over on to my front and supported myself above him on my elbows. He laughed more loudly.

'Go on – tell me,' I begged.

He rolled his head from side to side.

'Please – I won't tell anyone.'

He opened his eyes for a second and managed to control his laughter. He choked once, then spluttered.

'Did they?' I demanded.

He smiled. 'God knows.'

Nineteen

It was the sun streaming in through the window that woke me. For a couple of minutes I lay there motionless, letting consciousness gather momentum, gradually recalling all the events and emotions of the previous night. Then I turned towards him. He was still sleeping, snoring slightly, but peaceful; quite exhausted. I did not disturb him. I looked around the room. The brilliant rays of sunshine picked out the fluff and dust in shafts. They drifted down and up; I watched them dance, deciding what to do.

At last, as silently as possible, I slipped from the bed and started to dress. I had no idea what time it was; early, I knew, since it was so quiet outside; but I had made my mind. I wouldn't spoil it all by being there when he woke. I thought: let him remember those last few moments before we fell asleep. I was sure it was right. We would not meet again, but at least we had both survived. Something had come of it.

A short while later, now dressed, I tiptoed from the room, the door once more clicking behind me faintly. I walked quietly along the corridor and down the stairs. In the foyer the all-night porter, dozing uncomfortably behind his desk, opened an eye and winked at me. It was only 6 a.m. He knew who I was.

Twenty

When he awoke he stretched his arm instinctively across the
bed. She was not there. For a moment he was perplexed, and
then he understood. He looked faintly saddened but nevertheless managed a smile at his mistake, He yawned, looked at his
watch, seemed surprised to find how long he'd been asleep.

At last he got up. For a while he pottered round the
room – not doing anything of note, but slowly fixing where he
was; orientating himself.

Finally he went over to the desk and sat down. On his desk
were an ashtray and a paper-weight, a wad of papers covered in
scrawly writing, and a half-empty bottle of ink. His pen rested
on one side of the ashtray. There was nothing else.

He yawned again, then turned to that last page he had written
the night before. His eye travelled quickly over the words,
being familiar, now part of himself. At one point, he paused to
insert a comma, but otherwise concluded that it seemed all
right. There was only one line which he did not feel too happy
about. He read it once more:

We would not meet again, but at least we had both survived.

He slowly shook his head. For a moment he gazed dreamily at the window and drummed his fingers on the table. Then he picked up his pen and unscrewed the cap. At last his mind was made up. He swiftly crossed out 'would' and changed it to 'might'.